SOUND OF GUNFIRE

He was a young greenhorn, not even eighteen, when he saw too much. And they had to stop him talking — one way or another. So he went on the run for twelve long years, carving out a new life following the Texas cattle trails . . . But now the woman he had wronged has found him, all her long-held bitterness turned to hatred. And the vultures from his past swoop down once more, sending him running for his life from the sound of gunfire — again . . .

Books by Jake Douglas
in the Linford Western Library:

LAREDO'S LAND
RIO GRINGO
RIO REPRISAL
QUICK ON THE TRIGGER
A CORNER OF BOOT HILL
POINT OF NO RETURN
SUNDOWN
SIERRA HIGH
JUDAS PASS
LOBO AND HAWK
RIDER OUT OF YESTERDAY

JAKE DOUGLAS

SOUND OF GUNFIRE

Complete and Unabridged

LINFORD
Leicester

First published in Great Britain in 2006 by
Robert Hale Limited
London

First Linford Edition
published 2007
by arrangement with
Robert Hale Limited
London

The moral right of the author has been asserted

British Library CIP Data

Douglas, Jake
    Sound of gunfire.—Large print ed.—
Linford western library
1. Western stories
2. Large type books
I. Title
823.9′14 [F]
788 2855
ISBN 978–1–84617–585–5

Published by
F. A. Thorpe (Publishing)
Anstey, Leicestershire

Set by Words & Graphics Ltd.
Anstey, Leicestershire
Printed and bound in Great Britain by
T. J. International Ltd., Padstow, Cornwall

This book is printed on acid-free paper

1

Gunfire

Just like twelve years earlier, it was the sound of gunfire that set the whole thing rolling — again.

Clinton, scouting ahead of the trail herd, was in the foothills when he paused, cocking an ear to the distant crackling hammer-taps of gun shots. They were coming from the main range of the big divide and he had just found a canyon with water where the herd could rest for the night.

But way out here, in outlaw and Indian country, a man just didn't ride on with closed ears when he heard shooting that was obviously a gunfight in progress. He couldn't do much alone but he could get the lay of things and, if necessary, ride hell for leather back to the herd and get reinforcements.

This is what he did — though reluctantly. He had good reason to know that sometimes a man playing the good Samaritan could end up with the dirty end of the stick.

Still, he set the big, dusted grey over the rise and into the bigger hills towering above. It was a zigzagging climb and he half-hoped the shooting would have stopped before he got much further. But it continued — like someone driving in nails at random down the street.

Both Clinton and the horse were blowing when they topped-out on a crest and he hit the ground running, dragging his field-glasses with him. Stumbling, he sprawled and continued rolling behind a sun-hot boulder with peeling grey-green lichen. Knocking his hat back from his eyes, he focused the glasses on the scene below in a large flat grassy meadow that stretched too far between towering walls to be called a canyon.

There were three wagons down there

— immigrants making the trek to the Promised Land — and one of them had lost a wheel. The other two Conestogas had obviously stopped to lend a hand. And someone had taken advantage of the hold-up.

Riders were dodging in and out of the timber fringing the meadow, shooting into the wagons whenever they thought they had a target. A quick shift of the glasses and he could see that at least one immigrant was down, a couple of women working over him on the ground. The others returned fire from underneath and inside the box of the wagons. Five or six guns.

But they weren't doing much harm to the attackers. There seemed to be no more than half-a-dozen raiders but they knew what they were about. And they were white men, not Indians as he had half-expected.

Lips compressing, Clinton refocused, taking a slow sweep among the continually moving raiders. He even lifted his upper body a little, using his elbows to steady the glasses on one particular man.

'Goddamnit!' he breathed.

This was going to need at least half the trail hands to come back here and lend the wagoners a hand.

That was Shank Cutter's bunch down there.

★ ★ ★

'Shank Cutter?' echoed Drag Stanton, trail boss of this big herd on the way to railhead at Tucson. 'How you know?'

'Seen him.'

Drag, a man in his early forties who had seen just about all the wild trails had to offer, stroked his frontier moustache and put those horizon-set blue eyes on Clinton's square-jawed face. 'How do you *know*, Clint?'

Clinton seemed a little uneasy, but said clearly enough. 'Knew him one time — look, Drag, those folk don't stand a chance. Cutter and his men are experts at wearing down greenhorns

4

— and a lot of men who figured they were professionals, too. Shank rode with Quantrill and learned all the dirty tricks. We've got to get back there and help before they massacre everyone!'

Stanton kept his hard gaze on his scout and point rider. 'Just the big do-gooder from Texas, ain't you?'

'I'm not from — ' Clinton started to say, exasperated at the delay, but cut off the denial. 'C'mon, Drag! We'd be glad of someone coming to help us!'

Drag Stanton nodded, though there was some subdued query in the pinched blue eyes. 'Get Danno and six or seven men. I'll ride with you. Stitch and the others can handle the herd through here till we get back.'

Eight, possibly nine, men, thought Clinton as he hurried off, calling to Danno on the drag.

It might be enough — it better be. Because once Shank Cutter started a raid, all he left afterwards was a heap of dead men — or women.

★ ★ ★

The shooting was still crackling through the hills when they came over the crest where Clinton had dismounted to use his glasses. Most of the shooting now was being done by the riders at the edge of the timber. It meant either the immigrants were running low on ammunition and trying to conserve it or their numbers had been reduced by Cutter's bullets.

Drag, ex-army, made a couple of sweeping, cutting motions with his right arm. One to the right, the other to his left. 'Clint, take Peggy, Chance and Slats — Danno, you and the others come with me. You know what to do. Just remember that's Shank Cutter, accordin' to Clint, and he don't take prisoners; you know what I mean?'

They were hard trail men, used to fighting off Indians and rustlers, and some had seen plenty of bloody action during the war, but none of them looked too happy at Drag's remark, although all nodded that they savvied what he meant.

Shoot to kill.

They swept down the slope on the side away from the raiders, then went up-and-over in a hurry, whipping their mounts with rein ends and rowelling with spurs. They were skylined for no more than twenty seconds.

The raiders were too busy concentrating on the wagons to notice them and had no reason to even look behind. They had the upper hand here and they knew it: the wagon folk were getting worn down. There were two men down with womenfolk working over them now and three horses lying tangled in harness, another hip-shot and trumpeting wildly, rolling its eyes as it made desperate and futile struggles to get up.

'Why don't one of them immigrants put a bullet through its head!' muttered Drag Stanton angrily, as he led his group in but swung his rifle away from the wounded animal towards the raiders.

The horse would have to endure its agony a little longer: he might just need that extra bullet.

At a signal from Drag, both parties came in like the closing jaws of a pair of pincers, standing in stirrups, shooting fast, levers clashing, rifles snapping, the lead raking the ranks of the startled attackers.

Two men went down in the first volley. A horse reared, whinnying and unseated its rider. The man floundered, snatched up his fallen rifle, but Drag Stanton, teeth bared, rode him down, wheeling his snorting mount so that it stomped the man into the ground, even as he shot at another outlaw, but missed. Then something slammed into his saddle and staggered the horse. It went down sideways, and Drag leapt out of the saddle. He was dazed and groping for his rifle when an outlaw with chest-long beard came thundering in, his gun coming down to line-up on the trail boss.

Clinton slammed his own mount into the outlaw's and the horses were briefly tangled as the killer tumbled from the saddle. He lost his rifle but thrust to his knees and whipped up his six-gun — but too fast. He fumbled and the weapon fell from his hand.

Clinton leaned down, thrust his smoking rifle barrel almost against the man's chest and triggered. As the body was blown back, Clint wheeled aside, saw that Peggy was down and wounded and that his wooden leg had splintered — again. This would be the third time since they had started the drive out of El Paso ... Danno Magee had a six-gun in each hand, blazing, but the man he shot at, although doubled over his mount's neck, spurred away. A bullet caught the outlaw in the side of the head and tore him off the horse's back as if swept off by a low-hanging branch.

It was hard, fast, desperate riding through the timber, the outlaws on the run now, pursued by the whooping trail men. Clint saw Cutter, the man's long golden hair his trademark, flowing greasily over his wide shoulders. The scout rode after him: it was a long time since they had seen each other and none of the old hatred had been forgotten by either man.

Shank Cutter looked wild-eyed and desperate as he turned his head, reloading his six-gun by feel — and expertly, too. He had had a lot of practice at this; a lot.

'Last raid, Shank!' called Clinton, cursing himself for wasting a breath.

But his words carried to the outlaw leader and Cutter straightened, surprise clear on his dark, scarred face.

'By hell! You!'

Although his gun was only partly loaded, he snapped the gate closed and without hesitation triggered two shots at Clinton. The man was a good shot and one of the bullets punched dust from the shoulder of Clinton's jacket, touching his flesh hard enough to make him reel in the saddle and miss with his own return shot.

Cutter wheeled his horse around to face his pursuer, bringing up his smoking Colt, teeth bared. Drag Stanton, riding in, his gun lifting, suddenly slowed, blinking in disbelief as he saw Cutter, oblivious to everything around him — except Clinton. The killer was focusing all his attention on the scout and this left Drag Stanton dumbfounded.

Everyone knew that Shank Cutter had an infamous reputation for riding out and leaving his men to their fate when the chips were down, pulling every dirty trick in the book so as to save his own worthless hide.

And here he was, almost clear of the hampering closeness of the timber, on the way to freedom, yet deliberately turning to face down Clinton, both men clearly intent on killing each other.

As Drag watched, their guns lifted together and it was Cutter who fired first, but Clint swayed left and forward, dropping across his mount's arched neck, continuing the movement, lower and lower, sliding around and shooting under the grey's straining head.

They were two of the fastest shots Drag had ever heard — actually he thought there was only one at the time until, later, when they had examined Cutter's broken body, they saw that there were *two* .44 calibre slugs in the man's shattered chest . . .

The sound of gunfire drifted away across the meadow now and the surviving immigrants were cheering and calling out to their rescuers from the group of wagons.

Drag came back from examining Cutter's body as Clinton closed the loading gate on his Colt and holstered the weapon.

'You got him dead centre.'

'Right where I aimed . . . how many others did we get?'

'All of 'em. We got two men hit and Lacey lost his hoss as well.' Drag's gaze held Clinton's, as he nodded and started to turn away.

'What?' the scout asked carefully, checking his move.

'You said you'd 'seen' Cutter before.'

'That's right — he hit a herd I was with. Cal Masters', out of Missouri.'

Drag nodded. 'You *knew* Cutter.'

'I just said I saw him when — '

'*Knew him*, Clint — you had a score to settle. Why else would he, of all people, turn back from escape to try to nail you?'

Clinton didn't answer. 'Wagon folk are coming across to thank us.'

'Never mind them — what was between you and Cutter?'

Clinton shifted his grey eyes to the trail boss. They were bleak and steady. 'None of your business, Drag — you oughta know better than to ask.'

Drag grabbed Clint's arm as he went to move around him. 'Clint, you're scoutin' for me. I've knowed you a fair spell, but I dunno nothin' much *about* you. If you're gonna keep on ridin' for me, I need to know about you and Cutter.'

'Why? He's dead. He can't do anyone any harm now.'

'You're not dead.'

Clinton's eyes pinched down. He took a breath or two before answering. 'I ride for the brand, Drag, always have, you know that. I'm no danger to you.'

'Guess I know that, too, but I'd still like to know.'

'Let it go, Drag. Though I'll tell you this: one time I was in a real bad bind between a rock and a hard place. There was one chance to get out and it meant riding with Cutter to do it. I took that chance, but didn't stay long. Shank always said I run out and left him and his cronies to face a posse alone. Well, maybe my gun might've made a difference, maybe not. But I never went back and hadn't seen him since I looked through those field-glasses an hour or so back . . . '

Drag slowly examined the tall man's face and eased up on his grip, nodding. 'OK, Clint, it won't be mentioned again. Now let's see who saved . . . '

They started towards a group of sweaty, grimy men hurrying out from the wagons, trailed by three women, two in sun bonnets and long dresses, one hatless. Clinton slowed, and Drag frowned.

'Now what?'

'Nothing. Look I ain't much on being thanked, Drag. But I know a little about broken wagon-wheels. I'll take Mitch and see if we can get it fixed for these folk.'

'Sure — yell out if you need another hand.'

But Drag frowned a little more as Clint hurried away. It was almost as if the scout was trying to avoid meeting the grateful immigrants.

In moments, they were surrounding him and his men, thanking the trail men profusely, clapping them on the back and pumping their hands, inviting them 'to vittles'.

The two women in sun bonnets were work-haggard, weary and lined, but their faces were smiling and one even

15

brushed dry, wrinkled lips across Drag's gunsmoke-grimed cheek.

He seemed embarrassed and tensed a little as the third woman approached.

She was much younger than the others, and she had a fresh-looking face, as if it hadn't yet had a lot of exposure to the harsh climate of the frontier. Her skin was smooth and almost golden, her hair jet black, eyes a dark shade of green, although he had the impression they might actually change colour in different lights.

He hoped *she* wasn't going to kiss him — but she was looking past his shoulder as she offered a slim, firm hand and thanked him in a quiet voice.

'Who's that man, sir? The tall one wearing the leather chaps?'

Drag knew who she meant but turned anyway. 'Who? Clint? He's my scout and point rider . . . you know him?'

She hesitated, a small frown touching her brow and then she shook her head just once. 'No — no, I thought maybe

— No, I don't know him if his name's Clint, but just for a moment he looked like someone I knew — a long time ago.'

Drag thought she didn't sound too sure about that.

2

Mistaken Identity

'Trouble is you haven't been soaking your wheels.'

One wagoner had been killed by Cutter, but the remaining drivers, Haggerty and Milton, stared uncomprehendingly at Clinton as he pointed to the wrecked wheel and how the iron tyre seemed too large for the wooden rim.

'You've let the wheel dry out and the wood's shrunk away from the iron. The tyre came off when you hit a rock or a pothole, and then several spokes crumpled.'

Haggerty, a large man with a pot belly and powdersmoke still marking his sweating face, scratched at his hair which stuck out from his head like wire. 'No one never told us that! We were store-keepers before startin' this.'

Milton, smaller, but by no means a midget, hitched at his rope belt and scratched the end of his bulbous nose. 'You sayin' we oughta take off the other wheels and — soak 'em? In what?'

He looked around, sweeping an arm. There was no sign of water through the lush grass of the meadow.

'There's a stream ahead — go to the edge of the meadow, swing south-west — that's angling left — '

'We're not altogether dumb, mister!' growled Haggerty, but Clinton's expression didn't change, nor the easy note of his voice. He looked back towards the other wagons and the people moving about. His eyes seemed to search for something and then slid past the small figure of the girl with the raven-wing hair and settled on Haggerty again.

'Well, that's where you'll find a stream. Has a bed of pebbles which is just right. Drive your wagons there and make camp for a couple of days. Have to block your wagons so you can remove the wheels. Just roll 'em into the water and leave 'em to soak. Two-three days ought to do it.'

'OK — but what d'we do about this wagon with the busted wheel?'

'Be no problem if you'd brought a spare — didn't anyone suggest it to you?'

Haggerty shook his head. 'The agent took care of all the supplies and that stuff. Never mentioned a spare wheel.'

'Well, drive your wagons to the stream. Drag'll lend you men to help you get the wheels off. Soak 'em all except one, which you can roll back here and we'll fit it, get this wagon to the stream, too, and get its wheels in the water. Then I'll see about building you a new one to replace this.' He kicked at the pile of splintered wood lying mostly within the circle of iron. 'Lucky we'll salvage something. Spokes are easy enough to make, but the curve of the rim takes time.'

'What about the iron tyre? Won't that need to be shrunk or expanded or somethin'?' Milton had more of a grasp of details than the fat Haggerty and Clinton told him, yeah, they'd have to build a fire with a lot of heat, in fact, several fires around the circumference of the iron tyre, then fit it over the new wheel assembly and let it cool, when it would shrink onto the wood and hopefully clamp everything together firmly in place.

'Are you a wheelwright then?' Milton asked, and Clinton looked at him sharply, but seeming to realize it wasn't appropriate, grinned and shook his head.

'Worked for one once . . . '

Drag Stanton fretted some about having his men lend the immigrants a hand but knew it was necessary. While the wagons were moved to the stream and jacked up onto new-sawn blocks and the wheels were removed, Clinton and Danno Magee stayed behind and worked at jacking up the collapsed wagon. They used a long pole and rock as a fulcrum and struggled to hold the axle high while they pushed a length of tree trunk under. Their muscles were screaming by the time they managed it and they quickly sat down and had a smoke.

Then they started greasing the hub so it would be ready to take the wheel when it was rolled back from the stream.

The light was closing in when Mitch and Lacy dragged the wheel in across the grass behind their mounts: it was lush enough to let the wheel slide easily.

'Easier than rollin' the son of a bitch,' said Mitch, but Lacy, one arm bandaged from the gunfight, said sharply, looking about, 'Watch it! She can't be that far behind — might hear you cussin'.'

Clinton stubbed out his cigarette, asked, 'Who?'

'That young gal. She's bringin' you some cold cuts an' a pot of coffee. Well, we better get back for supper. You fellers aimin' on joinin' us or stayin' here tonight?'

'We're getting back to the herd soon

as we can,' Clinton said sharply. 'I'll have to ride back in the morning and rebuild that wheel . . . or Drag can do it. He knows how.'

Then they saw the girl coming, riding slowly with her bundle of food and a pot of coffee held precariously in one hand. Clinton jerked his head at Danno to go lend her a hand and the man went eagerly.

The other cowboys hung around, but Clinton could see it was only because of the girl, not necessarily to see if he needed help. Then he did a surprising thing.

He turned to the axle hub which was thick with black grease and grit, scooped off some on his fingers and smeared it across his face. Lacy's jaw dropped and he started to speak, but then the girl had arrived and was being attended to by the others. Lacy frowned as Clinton turned his attention to the hub. Twice he lifted his grease-smeared hands within thirty seconds, further smearing the grease across his face.

'You look like Cochise on the warpath!' opined Lacy, but then the girl came across with a paper-wrapped sandwich and a tin cup of coffee.

She frowned as Clinton went on working as if he didn't know she was there. 'Here's something to eat,' the girl said, in her quiet voice.

He nodded without looking at her. She was only small, no more than five feet three, he guessed. 'Thank you, ma'am.' He waved a grease-packed hand. 'I'll tend to this chore first and eat later.'

She set the food down, started to turn away, and then swung back. 'Clay? *Is* that you, Clay Selby . . . ?'

Hat canted down across his face whose lines were distorted and broken by the smears of grease, he glanced sideways at her, hands working on the axle hub by feel. 'Name's Clinton, ma'am.'

'But you look — so — like him! Oh, you're bigger, older than when I last knew him, of course. I mean, it was twelve years ago . . . '

24

He grinned, still not looking at her directly. 'Reckon I'd remember *you* from twelve years ago — and a lot longer'n that, miss.'

She might have blushed, but it was hard to tell in the fading light. 'Well, thank you, Mr Clinton!' She was still peering steadily at his half-hidden face, eyes narrowed.

'Just 'Clinton' or 'Clint' will do, ma'am. D'you have a name? Apart from 'ma'am'?'

She nodded solemnly. 'Of course. It's Cassie Bier — that's B-i-e-r — Not B double-e r.' Her gaze sharpened and she looked very closely at him as she added, 'This Clay Selby I knew, used to sometimes call me Short Beer, because I'm not very tall.'

'He wants a kickin' bad enough to keep him eatin' standing-up for a week if he couldn't think of something more romantic than that!' Clinton said, smiling, rubbing at the end of his nose and hiding even more of his features.

'Oh, he was very young then. Not

quite eighteen — I was a little younger, thought it was quite a smart endearment at the time . . . '

'Yeah, well, we're all a bit foolish when we're young, I guess,' Clinton said, turning back to the hub.'Danno, can you get that open-jawed wrench yonder? This nut's gonna take the two of us to get it off.' He glanced over his shoulder at the girl who was watching him closely.'Thanks for the grub, Cassie, let you know later what I think of it.'

'You're welcome . . . '

Feeling in the way now she moved towards her horse and Lacy doffed his hat with his good hand and offered to escort her back to the stream and the wagon camp.

She smiled distractedly and agreed. But she seemed a mite bewildered, glanced back several times.

After they had ridden off and Clint and Danno were struggling with the stubborn hub nut, Magee said, 'She's took a shine to you, Clint.'

26

'Nah — mistook me for someone else is all.'

Danno laughed and punched him lightly on the shoulder. 'Hell, man! How many times've you got to know a gal by tellin' her 'Ain't we met somewheres before, darlin'?''

Clinton smiled crookedly. 'Maybe you're right, but I don't reckon a Quaker gal would be so forward.'

Danno's face screwed-up. 'Quaker? Why the hell you say she's a Quaker?'

Clinton seemed to stumble over an explanation briefly, then shrugged. 'I dunno — she just has that look.'

'Yeah, well, she can make me quake in my shoes just by givin' me that up-from-under look she was givin' you!'

Clint frowned, staring at Danno for a long uncomfortable moment. 'C'mon! Get going! I want to finish this tonight!'

Danno looked offended. 'Well, pardon me all to hell!'

He threw down the wrench and stormed across to his horse where Mitch was drinking coffee.

'Goddamn sorehead!' Danno said, and when Mitch blinked at him, he jerked his head towards Clinton who was working away at the greasy hub. 'Hell with him!'

* * *

Drag Stanton drew deeply on the last of his cigarette, flicked the butt into the coals of the breakfast-fire beside the chuckwagon. He exhaled a plume of smoke as he looked up into Clinton's face.

'You told 'em you'd be back to fix their wheel.'

'I know I did — but country gets drier from here on in, Drag, and I'll likely have to ride a lot further to find decent water for the herd. We might have to drive 'em all night if I don't locate water till late. You know how to tyre a wagon wheel. I've made the spokes and there's only one rim curve left to shape. If I get goin' now, I'll be back early.'

Drag remained silent as Clinton rolled his gear and stowed it in his warbag, then hefted his saddle, calling to the wrangler to cut out his grey for him.

'She scared you that gal, huh?'

Clint made himself turn slowly. 'What?'

'The wagon gal — Cassie Bier. Danno and the others told me how you painted your face with grease.'

'The hell I did! Some of it got smeared on while I was working, any I put on deliberately was to feel for grit — Your face is more sensitive than your fingertips and grit plays hell with a hub bearing, you know that.'

Drag smiled faintly. 'Yeah, I've heard of wheelwrights and engineers doin' that kinda thing. But you're dodgin' that gal. Now, don't deny it, Clint! No skin off my hooter if you don't want her to know who you are — but she used a different name to the one I know you by.' The smile faded now. 'Mebbe it could be my business after all.'

'Take it from me, Drag,' Clinton told him heavily, coldly, 'it's not your business nor anyone else's but mine.'

'And Cassie Bier's?'

'Go to hell, Drag,' Clinton said, swinging down towards the rope corrals where the wrangler had his bay ready for saddling.

Drag Stanton scrubbed a hand down his stubbled face, looking thoughtful.

★　★　★

Clinton hadn't been exaggerating when he said the country would be drier from here on in and he might have to ride a long way to find water for the herd.

He rode well past noon before he found the first signs of a creek or river — a line of distant green trees that meandered across the land. Although he strained to hear he couldn't detect birdsong at this distance.

But the herd could never reach there by nightfall in any case. It would have to be a dry camp or — Drag's decision

— the cattle could be driven on through the darkness until they came to the creek, if there was one, or were within easy reach of it come sun-up. There was a half-moon tonight so Drag might decide to continue the drive. It was always a hassle, pushing trail beef at night, specially this far into the drive, weeks out of El Paso on a gamble and hearsay that Tucson was desperate for beef. Many of the steers had been rounded-up in harsh conditions and were used to long periods between drinks, but they had gotten used to more or less regular watering now and would be hard to handle.

After a smoke, Clinton mounted again, sat the ledge on a low mesa, using his field-glasses to study that meandering line of trees. It would save him time and a hot ride if he could find definite signs they followed a stream of some sort.

Yes! Birds. Clouds of them, whipping around in flights of hundreds, wheeling and diving and climbing with astounding precision with flashes of brilliant plumage — then settling down in several of the trees. Good enough for him. If there was that much birdlife, there would be other animal life, too, so there had to be water.

He bagged the glasses and set the weary bay back along the trail they had travelled.

He met the herd not long before sundown. Drag was already starting to get them settled for the night on sparsely grassed flats. Red-eyed from the dust and glare of the long, hard day, Stanton snapped at Clinton, 'The hell you been? These damn critters're actin'-up and if I read your ugly face right we ain't gonna get to water tonight.'

Clinton told him the location of the creek and the trail boss threw his hat on the ground in temper, just stopped himself from stomping on it.

'Dammit! They told us in Bisbee there'd be water every few miles!'

'Crossed two dry creekbeds, Drag — been a dry season, I guess. But there's a small meadow about four, five hours' drive from here. We could settle the herd there and it'd be only a couple or three hours drive to the creek if we start before sun-up.'

Stanton sighed, picking up his hat and dusting it off. 'Steers ain't gonna be the only ones actin'-up when I tell the crew we've got a night drive ahead of us.'

'They'll bitch, but you know they'll do it anyway, Drag. What's for supper?'

Drag tried a crooked smile, gesturing to the chuckwagon where there was a lot of clattering of pans and hoarse cussing. 'You game enough to ask Cookie, go right ahead — I'll get out the first-aid kit meantime.'

Clinton arched his eyebrows. 'Like that, huh?'

Drag lowered his voice. 'Wagon tipped over on a cutbank. Never heard such cussin' nor hope to again!'

'Might just wait and see what comes

outa the oven,' Clinton said slowly, then, acting casual asked, 'Wagons get away OK with that new wheel?'

Drag gave him a steady look, nodded. 'One of the women, Mrs Milton, was close to whelpin' and havin' troubles, so we got 'em underway quick as we could — they'll find a sawbones for her in Tucson, OK.'

Clinton nodded then started to speak, but changed his mind and Drag asked quietly, 'Why you look so relieved?'

Clinton shrugged elaborately. 'No reason — was just hopin' that gal wouldn't keep botherin' me, is all. I could see she wasn't convinced I'm not this Selby feller she mistook me for.'

He turned away to off-saddle quickly, as if avoiding having to look at the trail boss.

'You must look a lot like him . . . ' Drag allowed.

'How could she tell after twelve years?' Clint's voice was edgy, almost snappy. 'She said he was only a kid then

— Hell, he'd be thirty now! A man changes a lot in that period of his life.'

'You're about thirty.'

Clinton turned and set his gaze on Drag Stanton. He spoke slowly and deliberately. 'I'm thirty-two — and I've never heard of this Selby or this damn Cassie Bier, either. Ah, the hell with it, I am gonna ask Cookie what's for supper! I'm too blamed hungry to be standing round shooting the breeze over something that don't matter a damn anyway!'

Stanton watched him stride away towards the chuckwagon and said half aloud, 'Well, if it don't matter, you sure are riled-up, Clint, old pard . . . ' Then, louder, 'She was askin' me about you while I was fixin' the wheel.'

Clinton stopped dead, turned quickly. 'What'd she want to know?'

Stanton smiled thinly. 'Where you were from, how long I'd knowed you, that kinda thing . . . '

Clint waited and when the trail boss said no more, snapped, 'And?'

Drag shrugged. 'Told her the truth, that you'd been drivin' trail for me for five years — and before that I knew about as much about you as you can put in a flea's ear — and still leave room for a pair of ridin' boots.'

Their gazes met and held. 'Don't she know a man's business is his own out here?' Clint sounded almost — hurt.

'Reckon she does, but she seems desperate to find this Selby feller. Got the notion he'd done her a hurt way back and she's never got over it.'

'Hell! Pair of kids! Wouldn't know the difference between a hurt and — and — just something a man has to do, no matter what.' Clint swung away angrily. 'Damn fool women! They got their own notions of things and them same loco notions can destroy a man!'

He kept storming towards the chuck-wagon and Drag Stanton tugged at his moustache.

'Clint, ol' pard, you are ever a surprise to me . . . '

3

Hit the Trail

It took the herd another ten days before they reached Tucson.

The small river that Clinton had found was a tributary of the Santa Cruz and they turned north and found some of the roughest country they had encountered so far. The amazing thing was, a man could have ridden straight to Tucson in a day and a half, but fighting 1500 weary, cussed, longhorns over the same distance was no faster than a crawling baby.

Water was scarce and when they finally came to some decent grass and the big river, the Santa Cruz itself, Drag stopped for four days to let the cows settle down and fill their bellies before the final drive into town.

He rode in ahead to Tucson and

learned that the gamble had paid off: Tucson was desperate for beef. Three meat agents followed him back to the herd and vigorous bidding began on the spot.

'Luck's changing,' observed Clint, as the agents vied with each other on the price of the beef.

Drag nodded, obviously pleased with the way things were going. 'Played it smart — delayed in town and let drop that I was desperate to sell. Word got back to the agents and . . . ' He gestured to the men. 'They're pushin' each other's price up an' don't realize it. There'll be a bonus for the boys. That feller you know across the Border from El Paso, south of Juarez — reckon you could dicker with him for his herd so we can get it back here pronto before these folk have had enough Texas beef?'

'I could, I guess — if I was goin' back to Texas.'

Drag's good humour faded abruptly. 'What? You said you'd make this drive and come back to help me get another herd together. I'm countin' on you to convince that Mex *amigo* of yours, Clint! We can clean up big if he'll sell quickly. And you're the one can make him see things our way.'

Clinton scratched at his dust-choked beard. 'I know I said that, Drag — guess I could write a letter to him . . . '

'Hell! A letter don't cut nothin'! You need to be there.'

'Guess I'll hit the trail after pay day, Drag.'

There was a stubborn note in Clint's voice and Drag knew him well enough to realize it would be little use arguing. Then he said, a little viciously, 'That damn gal's got you buffaloed, ain't she!'

Clinton narrowed his eyes. 'Nothing to do with her — don't even know, nor care, where she is.'

Drag snorted. 'The hell you don't — well, I can tell you she's still in Tucson, ran up to me in the street and asked about you. She ain't forgot you, Clint.'

Clinton's face was impassive. 'That's her hard luck — I'll draw my time and ride out, Drag. I'll give you that letter to Carlos — '

'You know what you can do with your damn letter! I was countin' on *you*, Clint! You know them Mexes won't take no notice of a letter! You gave your word, damn you!'

Clint frowned. 'You're gettin' greedy in your old age, Drag. You're gonna make a good profit here. Going back for a second herd is a bigger gamble than this one was. They won't sell for the same price you'll get for these.'

'Then I'll drive 'em to Tombstone! But I've blazed that trail across to here and I aim to make all I can from it before others start followin' and flood the market — Don't you let me down, Clint!'

Clinton was surprised at the vehemence and unspoken threat coming from a man he had always thought of as more a friend than just a boss. 'I'm sorry, Drag, I have to this time. You know I wouldn't do it otherwise.'

'It's that blasted gal! I don't care what you say! You done somethin' to her and she's out to get you and you're showin' a yaller streak!'

Clint didn't like the way this was heading. He could swallow a lot of insults from Drag because he did feel guilty about going back on his word, but they were fast approaching the line where he couldn't — wouldn't — draw back any further.

'Drag, let it go. This is heading places neither of us want to go.'

'Damn you, Clint! This is the break I been waitin' for! I took this gamble and if it hadn't worked I'd be busted, but it *has* worked and I can follow through and I'll be set for life. I can buy me a good ranch, settle down, mebbe even find me a good woman ... Christ, man, I even thought you might come as my foreman!'

'Mebbe I would've, Drag, but I'm a drifter, like to keep on the move, you know that.'

Drag, face tight, nodded gently. 'Yeah! I'm beginnin' to see why, too — you're runnin'. From that little gal, Cassie, and Lord knows what else. Ah, I've suspected there was somethin' in your past, but I never let it bother me. Till now, when it's gonna cost me the kinda life I've planned!'

'Carlos will accept the letter I'll write him, Drag. But it's still up to him in the end whether he sells or not — '

'But if you were there you could help him change his mind!'

Clint stood tall, weary of this now, and more than a mite sorry things had taken such a turn. 'I'm not coming back with you, Drag. You don't want to pay me off now, you can send it on to somewhere I can pick it up — I'll write you where.'

He started to turn away and Drag Stanton grabbed his arm, maybe more tightly than he intended, but Clint had had enough, slapped the trail boss's gnarled hand free. Some of the crew noticed and began to close in, sensing a fight brewing here.

'Don't put your hands on me that way, Drag,' Clinton said quietly.

'No? How about *this* way?' And Drag swung, hard and fast.

Clint didn't think it would come so quickly and was slow in getting his head out of the way. Bark-hard knuckles slammed into the side of his jaw. He felt as if his lower face was coming adrift from his skull as he staggered. He stumbled, had to put a hand down quickly to keep from going all the way to the ground. Men shouted and came running as Drag closed and drove a knee into Clint's side, sending him sprawling.

Clint was raging when he bounded to his feet, ducked under the next punch and weaved, giving himself time to collect his spinning senses, ears ringing, jaw throbbing. He backed off and Drag came after him, swinging hard, grunting with the effort. Some of the punches landed and staggered the scout. Then he propped suddenly, had had enough of back-pedalling. He threw up a forearm that parried Drag's blow, ducked in and under, smashed a battering-ram fist into Drag's ribs.

The trail boss gagged and doubled over as he floundered back. Clint stepped after him, hooked a right and left against the man's contorted face, slammed him on the kidneys and drove him to his knees. He lifted his own knee into Drag's face and sent him sprawling. In the kind of rough and tumble that was a part of trail driving, he would normally have stepped in and used the boot, likely ending it here and now. But he didn't want this fight.

He had been hurt — and not just by Drag's fists — and he felt bad about going back on his word, but there was a lot the trail boss didn't understand. *One helluva lot!*

Clint wasn't about to explain and knew here was where a long friendship ended — had already ended. He reached out his right hand, offering it to the gagging, bloody Drag.

'C'mon, Drag, get on your feet and I'll ride out — this is as far as it needs to go.'

But Drag, noted for his meanness when his quick temper made him really riled, bared his teeth and came hurtling up, driving the top of his head into Clint's midriff. The scout grunted and went back with Stanton wrapping his arms about his hips, ramming his head again into his mid-section, ramming him over backwards. Short of breath and long on pain, Clinton writhed, collected two hammering blows, bucked wildly. The unexpected move caught Drag off-guard and he tumbled off Clint.

The scout rolled and drove both feet into Drag as he started up. Stanton went down, skidding, and Clint, ears roaring with pain and the shouts of trail hands, got unsteadily to his feet. The trail boss, slowed down some now, spun to hands and knees, thrust up with an audible grunt of pain and effort. His wild blow caught Clint as he ducked, skidding across the top of his skull. He reeled and Drag grimaced in pain, clutched his hand to his chest.

Clinton lunged in and hooked him on the jaw before he was fully straightened. Drag twisted and floundered and Clint went after him, set on finishing this now. His fist hammered the trail boss to his knees and the scout twisted fingers in the other's lank hair, yanked his head back, and drove a final, punishing blow into his face.

Drag Stanton jerked and flopped against Clinton who had his legs spread now for steadiness. He lifted a knee and Stanton fell backwards, sprawling, bloody, breathing stertorously. The men gaped — none had ever seen Drag Stanton lose a fight . . .

Clinton fought for breath, saw the meat agents also staring at him, and turned to the trail hands.

'I'm riding out. Tell Drag . . . I . . . I'll be in Tucson overnight . . . if he wants to . . . pay me . . . otherwise, I'll . . . write him from . . . somewhere.'

46

'Judas, Clint,' Danno Magee said, worriedly. 'I dunno what the blow-up was about, but — hell — don't just ride out! Drag wouldn't want that, no matter what!'

He looked to the others and several agreed with him. Clint shook his head, then Danno added, 'We wouldn't want it either, would we, fellers?'

They all agreed this time and Clinton smiled thinly. 'Sorry, boys — *muchas gracias*, but I've gotta go. See you through the dust of another herd sometime, some place . . . maybe. And we'll wash that dust away with a few dozen beers!'

The meat agents were still arguing about the top price they were prepared to pay when he rode out.

Drag Stanton was just coming round but Clinton didn't even slow down.

★　★　★

It took a while for Drag to come round properly and he was savagely angry when the men and even the sour cook tried to help him get cleaned up.

He looked down at his swollen right hand, saw he had popped a knuckle and stood still long enough for Cookie to put it back. It hurt like blazes and he allowed the cook to smear it with cooking fat and then to bind the hand firmly.

'Danno, fetch my rifle and tell the wrangler to get me a fresh horse.'

Magee hesitated. 'You ain't goin' after him, boss?' Drag glared impatiently. 'Hell, this is a bad thing, Drag. You and Clint — Judas, you been pards for years . . . '

'*Get me the goddamn rifle!*'

They knew there was no stopping the trail boss now. He was quick to anger and slow to forgive. They had seen it all before over the years. And he was deeply hurt.

Looked like this time it was going to end in a killing . . .

★   ★   ★

Clinton was stiff and already feeling the ache from the punishment he had received. It was a hell of a thing. About the last thing he wanted.

He had been too complacent, of course, after a few years of feeling settled on the Border, living mostly in Mexico among good friends, occasionally paying visits to El Paso and the Rio towns from time to time. Thought he had the thing licked. *Finally licked* . . .

Then that damn Cutter had to attack the immigrant wagons and one of the immigrants was Cassie Bier.

He still didn't know how he had managed to stay so calm, to deny her queries so coolly and with such a straight face . . . *Practice*, he guessed. He'd had plenty of that in the last twelve years. Mind, it had made his stomach lurch and his heart pound to see her again. She had grown into a fine-looking woman. He would've recognized her anywhere — just as she recognized him, but the grease on the face had helped to confuse her and undermine her confidence.

Now it was starting all over again, steam-rolling him into another flight to — God knew where this time! At least he could be thankful that it had been Cassie who had run him down and not some of Clutterbuck's killers . . .

God-*damn!* But he was riled that it had happened. Specially the bust-up with Drag Stanton. They had been good pards and there had seemed to be some kind of secure future for him there. Now . . .

Well, Tucson next stop and he had about two dollars and seven cents to his name. He hoped Drag would calm down, pay him off so he could be on his way. Maybe California or one of the north-western states — Oregon or Idaho. Close to Canada if he needed to run again.

He never heard the shot until after the bullet chewed hunks of bark from the trail-side tree, spraying him with sap and a few startled ants and other insects that had been living on the tree.

Instinct that he had honed over the years took charge. He rowelled with his spurs, slid down the side of the horse away from the direction of the bullet, clinging to the saddle horn with one hand, the other sliding his six-gun out of leather. Two more shots came to him faintly above the clatter of the mount's hoofs and he heard one ricochet from another tree. He couldn't see anyone behind or on the slope where he figured the rifleman would have to be. Yet another bullet whined off a hillside boulder and a following one dug up turf ahead of his horse.

It came to him then that whoever was doing the shooting wasn't trying to bring him down — the horse itself would be the best target if that was the purpose — but was merely trying to get his attention.

Well he sure had that, whoever he was!

Taking a chance, Clint slowly slid

back into the saddle, but kept crouching low. Then he tugged back on the reins as he saw the rider angling down the slope, rifle butt now braced against one thigh.

It was Drag Stanton.

A measure of the mistrust that had sprung up between them was the fact that Clinton didn't holster his Colt, but kept his thumb on the hammer spur as the battered trail boss rode up, the bandage on his right hand stark and white.

'Hold up, you jughead!' Drag called, reining down a few yards away. 'I was just tryin' to get you to stop.'

'Thought you were trying to stop me all right — permanent.'

Drag smiled crookedly. 'Started out that way, but maybe the wind from my racin' hoss cooled me down, blew some sense into me. Aw, hell, Clint, what happened back there? I mean — '

'You were right, Drag — the gal has rattled me. She's outa my past and I thought I'd shaken her and a lot of fellers who wanted to kill me long ago. I don't really have time to go into details.'

Drag held up his bandaged hand. 'I oughta known you'd have a good reason, but I was too damn hairtriggered to think straight, worried about what kinda price them meat agents are gonna end up with.' He sheathed the rifle, fumbled in his saddle-bags and brought out a small leather poke that clinked, tossing it awkwardly to Clint who caught it.

'Fifty bucks there — trail money. Won't need it this close to Tucson. I can give you a chit to hand to the banker in town. I'd ride in but I'd best not stay away from the herd until the agents gimme a price. Oughtn't to be standin' here shootin' the breeze even now . . .'

He tore a page raggedly from his sweat-soiled tally book and took a stub of pencil from his shirt pocket. Holding the pencil awkwardly because of his bandaged hand he wrote slowly, resting the page on his thigh. He handed it across and Clint saw the angled, childish script and scrawled signature.

'This is for two hundred dollars! Drag, I never earned that much, and counting this fifty you just gave me — far too much, man!'

'If you're hightailin' it, you'll need money. Some of it's for the years we've put in together, some — well, to make up a little for back there today . . . '

'Forget that. We were both fools.'

'And you'll be a bigger fool if you don't take what I'm offerin'.' Stanton set his mount alongside and held out his bandaged hand. 'Be gentle with me, sir — 'cause you got the hardest blamed head this side of the Rio!'

Clint grinned despite himself, took the hand in a gentle pressure, looking into Drag's face. 'Well, if it has to end — and it does — I'm glad it's like this, Drag. Luck, *amigo*!'

'Ride far and well, Clint . . . '

'Clay, actually — Clay Selby. From Long River, north of the Platte, Colorado.'

'Always suspected that Texas accent was phoney!'

Both men felt awkward now the moment of departure had arrived.

'Well, better hit the trail before Danno gives the herd away . . . You tell that banker I'll be depositin' several thousands with him if he fusses about payin' out on that chit.'

Clinton nodded and lifted a hand, watched Drag Stanton wheel his mount and spur back into the shadowed hills.

He turned his mount slowly, then lifted it to a lope, the poke of cash and the crumpled pay-chit in his jacket pocket.

With a little luck, he would get into town before the bank closed for the day, then he needn't even stay overnight.

He sure didn't want to run into Cassie Bier again.

4

Prisoner

The Tucson banker, a neat man with pomaded hair that filled his office with a cloying, flowery scent, poked at the grubby, torn tally-book page on his desk with a long pencil. Obviously he didn't want to soil his hands by picking it up.

He adjusted his glasses and squinted at it. 'I don't know this Drag Stanton or his signature, Mr — er — Clinton. I don't think I can pay you such a sum of money on the strength of this — er — note.'

Clinton was trail-dusted, smelled of sweat and horses, was weary and clearly marked from his recent brawl. He held down his irritation, though, and thumbed back his hat as he stood across the desk from the banker who

56

hadn't even asked him to take a seat.

'Banker, anyone from Texas to Nebraska knows Drag Stanton and that his word's good. True, this far west isn't his normal stamping ground, but he has fifteen-hundred head of longhorn steers camped outside of town, with three meat-house agents fighting to buy them. He'll be depositing thousands right here in your bank within a few hours.'

'Well, that's all very fine, but — look, why don't we wait until this Mr Stanton comes in and makes his deposit and then I'll have no problem meeting your request.'

'I'll tell you why, Banker,' Clint said, tight-lipped, seeing the frown and wariness come into the man's well-fed face at his tone. 'Because I have reason to quit early and I need to draw that money. Drag won't be in before dark, maybe not even till tomorrow morning — '

'Well, there you are. Have a night on the town while we're waiting. I could advance you, say, twenty dollars . . . '

Clint leaned his big, scarred hands on the desk edge and thrust his face towards the banker. The man reared back in his chair, looking thoroughly alarmed now.

'Mister, I want that money and I want it now — I'm in a hurry. Why, is my business. You got no worries about Drag honouring that chit, you got my word on that.'

The banker gave him a strange look and Clint almost smiled.

'OK, I look like a saddle tramp and that's what I've been for the last several weeks, all the way from El Paso, eating the dust of that big herd. But I scrub up pretty good — if you're the kind of feller who puts a lot of stock in a man's appearance.'

'In the money business, Mr — er — Clinton, first impressions count.' He drummed surprisingly slim fingers, one sparkling with a gold ring set with some kind of jewel, on his side of the desk. 'All right, suppose I advance half of this amount and you undertake to stay in town until Mr — er — Drag arrives and deposits his beef money? Agreed?'

'No, dammit! I want the full two hundred dollars so I can be on my way!'

He had instinctively dropped a hand to his gun butt and he saw the blood drain from the moon face. The man ran a bright pink tongue around his blubbery lips.

'Er — I should point out that we have a tough sheriff here in Tucson!'

'The sheriff don't need to come into this, for Chris'sakes!' Clint rapped a stiffened finger onto the grubby, torn paper, realizing how it must look to the banker, although bankers in trail towns likely wouldn't think twice about it. But for this man, dealing with a Texas trail driver was a new experience. 'Two hundred, Banker! *Now!*'

The man nodded jerkily, demanded Clint's signature on a receipt, and got him the money. Clint put it away in his jacket pocket and nodded.

'Thanks for your co-operation, Banker.

Relax, you won't lose a red cent on the deal.'

'I should hope not!' He was sweating profusely now, but was damned if he was going to reach for his silk kerchief and mop his face in front of this Texas hardcase. 'I've already warned you about our sheriff.'

'So long, Banker.'

Clinton was smiling to himself as he left, stalled his horse in the nearest livery and went in search of a bath house.

He was soaking in the suds up to his ears, eyes closed, almost asleep, when he heard the door of the room open. He started to sit up straight, glancing at his six-gun on the chair he had placed close to the tub.

Two men entered, one with a cocked six-gun, the other holding a big Ithaca shotgun, both hammers notched. The one with the six-gun was short, dressed neatly enough although his clothes looked as if they had seen a lot of use. Grey hair showed beneath his hat which, for some reason, was held on his head with the tie-thong hooked under his clean-shaven chin. As he rolled across the room, moving stiffly, Clint saw the brass star on his soft-leather vest.

'You be a man called Clinton?' he asked, and there was some kind of foreign brogue deep in there, Scottish or Irish, Clinton wasn't familiar enough with it to say for sure.

'I'm Clinton.' His right hand, dripping suds, was poised about six inches from the butt of his Colt.

'Just set that hand on the edge of the tub, laddie,' the sheriff said, and the other man, lanky, craggy-faced, sporting a deputy's star on a soiled shirt front, moved around and used the long barrel of the shotgun to ease the chair back out of Clinton's reach.

'You received a couple hundred bucks from the banker an hour or two back.' Clint nodded warily. 'Then you're our man. Get dressed.'

'What's going on? That banker didn't

like the look of the chit I gave him, I know, but it's genuine, and I told him Drag would be in later to deposit several thousand at his damn bank . . . '

The sheriff shook his head slowly. 'You know that isn't going to happen, son.'

Clint frowned, a suddenly cold jiggling stirring his belly. 'The hell it's not! Drag was just waiting to agree to a price the meat agents were haggling over and then he'd be driving in the herd, or at least bringing in his crew tonight and maybe the cows tomorrow . . . '

The lawman's fairly amiable face was hard. He shook his head once, sharply. 'Don't try to hornswoggle me, boy!' The accent made it sound like *harnswargle* but Clint got the meaning. 'You know well Mr Drag Stanton won't show up here or anywhere else, tonight, tomorrow, the next day — nor *ever again*!' He leaned forward and slapped the startled Clinton across the soapy face with an open hand. 'Because you murdered him for that poke and, being the greedy wee bastard you are, faked his signature on a filthy piece of paper that you used to extort two hundred dollars from our banker!'

Stunned, Clinton could only blink.

Then the deputy placed a foot against the tub and tipped it over, spilling the naked Clinton out with gallons of sudsy water that flooded across the room. The sheriff danced, swearing as he tried to keep his boots from getting wet.

Then the shotgun muzzles rammed against Clinton's back and the deputy growled, 'Get dressed, you murderin' son of a bitch! An' I won't mind a bit if you want to gimme trouble so I got an excuse to blow your goddamned leg off!'

★ ★ ★

It looked bad.

Danno, worried about the length of time Drag Stanton was away, and knowing how savagely angry the man had been when he rode out, went looking for the trail boss. He was urged on by the meat agents who wanted to make their final offer and get back to Tucson.

Danno found Drag at the foot of the slopes near a bullet-marked tree, shot to death, an ugly end for the Texas trail boss. The meat agents had witnessed the fight between Clinton and Drag and seen how the fury-driven trail boss rode hell for leather out of the camp with blood in his eye.

They insisted the only thing to do was call in the Tucson sheriff, a man of considerable reputation in the south-west, name of McVittie. Danno and some of the trail hands didn't want that right away — they felt it couldn't be the way it appeared. But the sheriff made a few enquiries, learned about Clint's somewhat hostile visit to the banker. Asking around town he learned that earlier in the day, Drag had bought some cigars to hand out after the sale of the herd. He had signed an I. O. U. for the storekeeper, who was obviously more trusting than the banker, and a comparison between this signature and the ragged, barely legible one on the old tally-book page didn't match up very closely.

'Some parts look alike, but mostly it's a pretty crude attempt to forge Mr Stanton's name,' Sheriff McVittie told Clinton through the bars of the cell in the rear of the jailhouse.

'Hell, Drag hurt his hand busting me on the head,' Clinton said, by way of explanation and saw by the lawman's face that he was only digging his grave deeper. He sighed. 'Yeah, we had a — difficulty just before I left the camp, but Drag came after me and patched it up, made out that chit on a page torn from his tally-book. His hand was bandaged and he was writing with it resting on his thigh.'

'You're a fly wee bastard, are you not, Clinton!' growled the lawman, shaking his head. 'There were marks where there'd been a gunfight — maybe you only winged Stanton, or drove him off somehow, but caught up with him again. Because there's powder burns on his body in two places which means a gun was pressed right into him to make sure he was killed!'

Clinton stared back, frowning. 'We shook hands,' he said carefully, slowly, holding McVittie's cold gaze. 'He even asked me to be careful because his hand was sore — we parted friends! He gave me that poke with the fifty dollars, then wrote out the pay chit.'

'For two hundred dollars? Man, I've been in a lot of trail towns and I never heard of any rider making two hundred and fifty dollars on such a short drive!'

'Hell, you think it was easy, comin' across from El Paso? No one's ever done it before. It was damn hard work and we went hungry and thirsty. Besides, Drag said he wanted to make up for the little fracas we two had had.'

'You've got an answer for everything,

have you not!' The sheriff was angry now, and it strengthened his accent. He shook a finger through the bars and for one wild moment Clint almost grabbed it and twisted it hard enough to snap. 'Well, you're just a durty, murdering, wee, sneaky bastard as far as I'm concerned and, though I didna know Drag Stanton, I'm going to see your carcass swinging from that cottonwood right outside! I canna abide greed or treachery, specially not when they're both linked! You're hellbound, Clinton! Get yoursel' used to the idea!'

He stormed off and Clinton stayed at the bars, gripping them until his knuckles were white, wondering how everything had suddenly blown up in his face.

And, more importantly, who *had* killed Drag Stanton after he had left him on the trail to Tucson?

He hadn't heard any shots, but if the murder gun had been rammed against Drag's body before firing, he wouldn't have . . .

But why? Just to frame him? Then the next question had to be — *who?*

*   *   *

The sheriff allowed Danno and Lacy and Mitch to visit him briefly just after dark. They were all at a loss to explain away Drag's murder and it boosted Clint to see that none of them believed he had done it.

'See any strangers hanging around?' Clinton asked, but they shook their heads.

'Too busy keepin' the herd together,' said Danno. 'There ain't a lot of grass left — anyway, the agents want it brought in tomorrow.'

'What'd they offer?'

'Twenty-one dollars a head.' Clint snorted and Danno added quickly, 'I said we wanted twenty-five minimum, but they said that's the highest they'll go.'

Clint shook his head. 'They'd go to thirty if you push 'em! They're *aching* for good beef here — Anyway, are you acting for Drag, or what?'

Danno looked embarrassed. 'Well, I din' know what to do, really, so I wired Drag's lawyer in E1 Paso.'

'Loftus? Yeah, that was a good idea, but keep at him. He takes on too much damn work, but tell him he's gotta make time for this, get it settled so everyone can get paid.'

Mitch said quietly, 'Don't look as if it's gonna concern you, Clint.' He gestured to the cell and the hard-eyed deputy standing just inside the passage door.

'Shut up, Mitch!' snapped Lacy, and Danno glared angrily.

'No, Mitch's right, Danno, I can't do anything from in here. Sheriff's keen to hang me. Said I'll be tried tomorrow.'

Danno glanced at the deputy who was watching closely. 'We been thinkin' on how we can get you out, Clint,' he said, in a low voice, 'but this McVittie seems to be hell on a walkin' stick.'

'A *what?*' asked Clinton, blinking.

'You notice the way he walks, slow and shufflin'? Arthritis, everywhere but in his gun-arm, they say — and he's got a bolt of lightnin' there. There's a lot of stories about him.'

'I've heard 'em, even down in Mexico,' Clinton admitted. 'Don't tangle with him, boys. I'll get outa this somehow. Obliged for you coming in.'

'Time's up!' bawled the deputy, waving the shotgun. 'Get out — *now!*'

'Kinda subtle, ain't he?' remarked Danno, as they turned to leave.

Clint smiled, but knew he had been too confident when he had said he would get out of this. The way things looked, the only way he'd get out of here would be at the end of a rope.

He rubbed his throat involuntarily, swallowing hard.

★　★　★

He was mighty surprised when Sheriff McVittie allowed him one more visitor — it must have been nine o'clock by then and he could hear sounds outside that told him Drag's crew were holding a wake, or just letting off steam in town. The agents would've advanced some pay, most likely.

But the biggest surprise came when he saw his visitor . . . Cassie Bier.

She wore a long blue dress with white lace across the bodice and at her throat. There was a gold necklet chain showing also, and she had on a small bonnet with the ribbon tied under her chin, black hair glinting in the lantern light where it spilled out from under the cloth. She held an oval tapestry handbag in both hands and gave him an almost shy look.

'I'm sorry things've gone so — wrong for you — Clay.' There was a tight, breathless edge to her words.

He didn't deny the name now, although he hadn't owned up to it to anyone else except Drag just before they parted.

'Not your fault, Cassie. I wondered if

you'd moved on or were still here in town.'

'Oh, yes. I decided to stay. The others went on after Mrs Milton gave birth. I'd planned to go all the way but — ' She tilted her jaw a little at him. 'But after I saw you with that trail herd . . . I couldn't settle! I *knew* you were Clay Selby although you denied it. And I wanted to get one more good look at you — preferably without all that grease smeared on your face.'

He smiled. 'Fooled you that time, huh?'

Her green eyes narrowed. 'You admit it now? You — you are Clay Selby?'

He shrugged. 'Doesn't seem to be any point in denying it now. Not when the future looks so . . . short.'

She impulsively reached up to the bars where one of his hands rested and closed her fingers over his, looking into his face. 'Oh, Clay! The number of times I've thought about you over the years! Not just thought about you, but *worried* — yes and *hated* you, too! For

72

running out on me the way you did!'

'Not the time or place to go into that now, Cassie, but I ask you to believe that I had no choice. I'd be dead long ago if I'd stayed.'

'Clay — I — I knew you must've been in some kind of terrible trouble, but — ' She suddenly stamped her foot. 'Couldn't you at least have *written!* Given me the courtesy of an explanation? That was what I found most unforgivable.'

She was becoming agitated now although he could see she was making an effort to keep control. He recognized that cold anger he had seen displayed once or twice long ago. He hadn't liked it then and he didn't like it now.

'No, Cassie, I couldn't've written. It might have led certain people to where I was hiding. And they'd've killed me between mouthfuls of food and then called for a second helping.'

She stepped back, face cold. 'You don't have to exaggerate — you have my full attention!'

'No exaggeration, Cassie — but leave it. I'm truly sorry for what I must've put you through. It's way too late for me to ever try to put things right I know — '

'Yes, it is!'

'If it's any consolation, I've never forgotten you, Cassie. Sometimes, riding nighthawk, alone with the cattle and the stars, I'd think about how it might've been with us, if I hadn't walked into all that trouble . . . '

She studied his face close-up through the bars and the deputy called it was just about time for her to leave. She waved without looking at the man, staring deep into Clint's eyes.

'I think I believe you, Clay!' she said huskily, a tremor in her voice now. 'When I hear you say . . . that! But I don't think I'm ready to forgive you — even after all these years. *Wasted years!* And for it all to end like this! Oh! It's not *fair*!'

'Fair or not, lady,' bellowed the deputy coming slowly down the passage now, 'it's time for you to go. Right now!'

She acknowledged with a nod, waving to keep him from coming any closer. Then said into the cell, 'Clay, come closer — quickly! Before he comes . . .'

He stepped forward and she reached through the bars, hand going out to touch his face. Suddenly she swung it as hard as she was able in the awkward position and it smacked him across the mouth in stinging pain. He reared back blinking. The deputy laughed.

Cassie's eyes were narrowed, her small mouth tight, bosom heaving with emotion. 'I'm glad they've caught you! I don't care what your excuses are for having run out on me, but I just want you to know that I'll be right in the front row when they march you up to the gallows! I *despise* you, Clay Selby!'

The deputy reached for her arm and began to drag her down the passage. 'She's ready to rip your eyes out, drifter!'

The stunned Clinton reckoned the same thing.

Then just to drive another nail into his coffin she said with cold satisfaction, 'I've wired that federal marshal, Clutterbuck. He might get here before they hang you. If he does, I'm sure he'll be only too glad to help slip the noose over your head!'

And then she was gone and he felt numbed, empty, with a nervous longing that began to shake his entire body.

He wondered if she knew Clutterbuck was the double-crossing son of a bitch who had set the killers on him in the first place! Hell, would she even care?

Slowly, he returned to the bunk, rubbing at his still stinging face: she might be small but she had plenty of power in those arms. He stretched out, staring up at the dark ceiling, soon shifting his gaze through the high set bars of the window where he could see a small section of brilliant stars.

Probably the very same ones that

were shining on the mine twelve years ago . . .

He remembered looking up at the stars as he hurried across the broken ground to the mine-shaft entrance, clutching the urgent wire that had just come through . . .

5

The Drunken Lady

It was a good job for a healthy young lad of seventeen, working as a trainee telegraphist for Western Union. Clay Selby had been more or less pushed into the position at the insistence of his father who saw stability and long-term security in the telegraph company.

Clay wasn't all that keen, although he had always had a fascination for advances in the various sciences. And using a telegraph key, sending messages down thousands of miles of copper wire, stretching from east to west, held a strong appeal to an imaginative young man, especially as the skill of the flicking wrist and the rattle of the brass key were absolute mysteries to the uninitiated.

Fortunately, Clay Selby had a knack

for learning fast and soon he was following closely behind the Key Masters, as the old hands were called — a name thought up by one of the men themselves, some folk maintained. But that's what they were — masters of their trade. And Selby's teachers showed a lot of interest in him as a star pupil because of his ability to learn and retain the knowledge: trainees rarely showed such apititude. Pay wasn't much but that would change dramatically once he became fully qualified.

But he needed experience, so they soon shipped him out of the Denver main office to some of the outlying telegraph stations: being transferred to far-off frontier towns was something Selby looked forward to.

At the end of his first year, he was given the job of 'relieving telegraphist' in a town called Patchett, south of the Raton Pass, New Mexico. It was a medium-sized town, the country around it producing both cattle and copper. In fact there was only one copper mine producing now, on top of the eroded hill at the southern end of town, called, of all things, The Drunken Lady. It had the only operating stamp mill and refining plant in the north of New Mexico. A big Denver syndicate controlled the mine which was in almost constant trouble with local cattlemen because sulphate run-off from the plant was sometimes washed by rains into the river used by the ranchers. Their productivity entitled them to some protection from such claims — but only while certain men held certain influential positions in government.

The story went that the mine site itself had been located by a mineral surveyor who had fed alcoholic drinks to a married woman and then brought her out to the hill so as to complete his seduction. She complained about lying on something sharp which he obligingly removed from under her naked pink buttocks — and later, in the light of dawn, while looking for his discarded clothes, he found the rock and recognized the green streaks in the ore as high-grade copper. He took out a claim and frivolously named the mine The Drunken Lady. But the lady did not regard it as an honour or see any humour in his choice, and demonstrated her feelings by shooting him through the buttocks. Some said she was a little off-target, because the terrified surveyor had turned just as she fired. He quickly sold out when the syndicate made an offer.

Neither he nor the woman were heard of again but the syndicate made it clear right from the start that they aimed to make a big profit as quickly as possible. If the townsfolk thought they were going to have new employment opportunities here, they were mistaken.

This syndicate had tentacles all over the south, stretching all the way to the Rio, and the majority of the men they employed were illegals from Mexico. Highly illegal, of course, but there were ways of ensuring officialdom turned a blind eye to such breaches of the Law.

But things change, including the men in high places. And just before Selby was stuck with the nightshift on the Patchett station, there was an election and a new head of Territorial Administration moved into the top position, despite a lot of political graft on the syndicate's behalf. This man let it be known that every business, every citizen of New Mexico from here on in would obey all laws and ordnances of the territory. He established a special force to police and enforce these laws.

He was especially down on exploitation of cheap labour and, one of the syndicate's friends still in a position to have inside information, sent an urgent wire to The Drunken Lady manager marked 'For immediate delivery night or day'.

Selby thought it was innocuous enough when the message came through: it simply said:

Mine inspection imminent.
Take necessary steps to ensure
compliance soonest. C.

He had no idea who or what 'C' was but that didn't matter. He looked at the old wooden-cased cottage clock ticking away on the wall with muted hammer-like strokes. Lord! Ten o'clock — the manager of the mine was going to love being disturbed at this time of night!

But he was alone and wouldn't change shifts with the head operator till 6 a.m., so he took a copy of the message, sent the code for 'Temporary shutdown', locked the door of the station and hurried towards the mine.

It was a nice night, the moon casting its strengthening glow behind the hill as it began to rise, a wilderness of several million stars twinkling above. The town was reasonably quiet, quiet enough to hear a woman singing in the Bijou theatre on Whipple Street. He had tickets to see the visiting company's show there for next week. He would be taking Cassie, of course.

It was pleasant, thinking about her as he slogged up the hill to the mine, the clanking of the ore-stamp mill growing louder as he approached. She was a lovely girl, the best thing that had ever happened to him, he admitted, smiling to himself. She knew her own mind, that little gal, and told him straight out that they were going to be married as soon as she was twenty-one — or sooner if she could work on her Quaker father enough to give his permission for an earlier wedding. Or they could elope! They even planned a 'theoretical' elopement, but both were privately considering putting their plans to the test of reality.

'Where you think you're goin'?'

The hard voice startled young Selby and he jumped as the guard on the mine gate stepped out of the shadows. He stammered out his business, clearing his throat.

'Judas! The boss ain't gonna be pleased about this — I'll find someone to take it to him. I ain't gonna be loco enough to do it myself this time of night. Gimme that wire!'

Selby snatched the yellow form in its ivory-coloured sealed envelope out of the man's reach, shook his head. 'I have to deliver it myself — company rules: urgent messages must be delivered by a Western Union employee and signed for — see? This here's the receipt book.'

'Suits me — you can take the blast for disturbin' the boss.'

Clay nodded and stepped through, making towards the darkened house silhouetted against the stars.

'Hey! He ain't up there — some sort of inspection's on in the old south twist shaft. Think they're gonna close it off completely for safety, blast in the entrance yonder, that one with the timber piled beside it. Might find a candle inside, otherwise you'll likely see a glow from where the boss and the others are.'

Selby found his way in, smelled the dank air. Not being a smoker at that time, he had no matches with him and felt warily along the wall as he made his way forward. As the guard had said, he could see a faint glow ahead and below, around a bend in the descending tunnel. He didn't care much for this place: *taking him closer to Hell*, he thought.

Voices drifted up, low-speaking American, and high, panicky Mexican. He knew a little Spanish and stopped, listening closely now.

'But, *señor*, we have give you good service! You say you return us to our homes when we finish! Now you say we must stay longer and work some more — is not fair, eh?'

'You made a contract,' a tired-sounding voice said, and Selby thought he recognized is as belonging to Tate Hannigan, the tough manager. 'Not our fault if you don't read the fine print, eh, boys?'

There was brief, hard laughter and more panicky shouts by the Mexicans, obviously eager to see their families again. By now Selby was at the bend, sliding silently along the wall, heart hammering. He risked a quick look around the corner.

A dozen ragged Mexican miners huddled together in front of a mineface that looked as if it hadn't been worked for years. There were a couple of oil lamps burning as well as candles on iron spikes driven into the earthen walls.

Four Americans stood facing the Mexicans — covering them with their guns. One man had a shotgun and Selby drew in a sharp breath as he recognized Hannigan, who said, 'OK, it's growing late and I'm tired. Time to stop all this hogwash and tell you the truth.' He bared big teeth in his large, horse-like face. 'It's a joke, *amigos*! Just a joke. Thought you'd appreciate it . . . but looks like you've lost your sense of humour.'

All the Mexicans looked towards one man, obviously their leader. He was tall for a Mexican, but rail thin. He blinked puzzledly. 'A — joke, *señor*? A joke mean something fonny, eh? But this is not fonny — The guns! The way these men beat us and push us down here!'

'Ah, hell!' said Hannigan suddenly, turning to the Anglos. 'Knew I shouldn'ta bothered! They just don't see anythin' funny in it at all.'

'We could show 'em in a way they'd understand, boss,' suggested a big man with black shirt and hat and stringy straw coloured hair hanging to his shoulders. Selby knew he was called Rush Landers — a hired gunfighter. He was only a little older than Selby, but looked cold and murderous, a born killer.

'Rush, I b'lieve you've found the solution,' Hannigan said, barely able to keep a straight face. He looked at the worried Mexicans. 'Just so's you know, *amigos*: you ain't wanted no more. *Comprende*? Outlived your usefulness. See, the new administration is jumpin' on anyone usin' illegals, and it's only a matter of time before they check us out.

We're gettin' in first, *jumpin' the gun, you might say.*' He laughed briefly. 'Truth is it's too much damn trouble sendin' you gabby bastards all the way back below the Rio, so we figured you oughta stay here.'

'Here, *señor?* What can we do here?' the tall one asked without real enthusiasm, looking distinctly worried.

Hannigan grinned and raised the shotgun. 'Tell you what you can do, *amigo* — *muchas gracias*, for asking — what you can do is to *die*! Right here and now. Then we'll blow the shaft in on top of you and no one'll know you were ever here. You'll have real peace for eternity. OK?'

The Mexicans panicked and the gunfire boomed and thundered through the tunnel, lighting it with bright flashes. Selby clapped his hands over his ears — blotting out not only the sound of gunfire, but the screams of the dying Mexicans, too. A choking cloud of powdersmoke made him cough and stung his eyes. He staggered away from the wall, a deafening ringing in his ears, and the murderers saw him.

Landers shouted, 'It's that kid from Western Union!'

'He's seen everythin'!' someone else said, hoarsely.

They began to reload frantically, but Selby was no longer in view now. He plunged back around the bend and raced up the incline of the tunnel, stomach wrenching, hearing shouts behind him. These were soon drowned in the crash of gunfire and bullets screamed off the walls, floor and roof as he ran on, covering his head futilely with his arms.

All he wanted was to reach that pale arch that seemed to be miles ahead, framing a hatful of brilliant, beckoning stars.

'Stop that goddamn kid!' roared Hannigan. His shotgun thundered and Clay Selby sobbed in fear as something shredded one side of his corduroy jacket, tugging violently and forcing him to break stride. But he pushed off the wall, banging his head and feeling the skin tear. Warm blood trickled into his left eye as he stumbled and half-scrambled, half-ran towards the entrance like a scuttling crab.

He made it out into the night and saw the gateguard standing at the foot of the slope now, rifle in hand, looking bewildered. He started to lift his gun as he saw Selby, who scooped up a large clod of compacted earth and hurled it viciously. To his surprise, it hit the man in the head and burst in a shower of gravel and dirt. Clay jumped over the falling body, snatched the rifle instinctively from the man's limp hands and zigzagged his way to the gate.

Panting, a stitch in his side making him grimace, he lurched against the gate post for support, fumbled up the rifle as he saw the dark shapes pouring out of the tunnel mouth. They began shooting as they ran towards him.

One other thing he had learned well since coming out west besides how to work a telegraph key at top speed, was how to shoot. One of the old Key Masters had originally been in the army and got Clay interested in firearms, taught him a lot of tricks of the trade.

'Wild country, this, boy — Injuns like our copper wire and cut it down whenever they can. You might have to go chase 'em sometime — or need to go hunt up a deer for grub out on one of the isolated stations. It's never wasted time learnin' how to shoot and to do it proper . . . '

Clay was an apt pupil and a straight-shooter.

He threw the rifle to his shoulder now and began to fire, bullets spurting gravel and puffs of dirt around the running feet of the men who wished to kill him.

It stopped them, surprised as much as afraid. But they shot back and bullets splintered the gate in several places and Clay dropped to one knee, fired until the rifle was empty. One man was down, screaming, clutching a shattered knee. Another had a hand clawed into his bleeding upper arm — he thought it was Rush Landers. Hannigan and the others who were unhit ran back into the mine. Hannigan paused before entering, blasting with both barrels of the shotgun.

The buckshot peppered the gate and splinters stung Selby's face. He dropped the rifle and charged through the gate, racing downhill through the night, still afraid for his life.

He had seen too much. With his knowledge he could close down The Drunken Lady, see Hannigan and Rush Landers and his friends hang for cold-blooded murder.

For their own safety they *had* to kill him, that was sure as sunrise. And they would — if they could catch him.

★   ★   ★

He knew there was no use approaching the local sheriff — he was Hannigan's brother-in-law.

But all Western Union telegraphists

93

were given a special code for contacting a federal marshal should one be required urgently for some reason. Sweating profusely, shaking like a bush in the autumn northers, Clay Selby stopped at the telegraph office long enough to tap out the code for the nearest US Marshal who had a base at Fort Union near Mora. He gave co-ordinates for a rendezvous, and a time, grabbed a horse and his own rifle. He hightailed it away from Patchett as riders thundered into Main and headed for the darkened telegraph office.

Clay figured he died a dozen deaths that night as he made his way across country, thankful for all those leisurely, exploring rides he had taken with Cassie when they had been seeking solitude so they could share their dreams without embarrassment — and do some courting in private.

He wound his way through heavy timber, climbed narrow trails to precarious lookouts from which he saw the riders, distant and ghostly in the moonlight, searching for his tracks. Hope began to send warmth surging through him. He wheeled the lathered mount, climbed over the mesa north of Wagonmound and made his way down to the rendezvous, hoping the marshal had received his frantic wire.

He had got it, all right, and kept the rendezvous.

'Name's Guy Clutterbuck, boy,' the large man in the shadow of Big Bear Rock called. 'What kinda burr you got under your saddle that you drag me out here this time o' night?'

Swallowing, voice shaking, Clay blurted out what he had seen and sat hearing his own ragged breathing for a long time before the marshal spoke. 'Well, that sure is a serious allegation, boy.'

'It's not an allegation! I'm reporting what I saw!'

'Sure you are, and I b'lieve you — know why?'

Selby, too tired to answer, merely shook his head.

''Cause I'm the man supplies them

Mexicans to Tate Hannigan.'

The shock anchored Clay to his saddle and maybe Clutterbuck had counted on that sudden freezing up as he brought up his six-gun almost casually and fired twice.

Selby reeled, caught the horn and clung on, but already he was raking with the spurs and the weary horse reacted by pure instinct. It leapt forward, crashed into the half-hidden marshal with enough force to set the lawman's horse whinnying wildly as it half-reared, lost balance and toppled sideways.

Clay unshipped his rifle and fired three fast shots, knowing he had at least killed Clutterbuck's horse. He saw that the man's leg was caught under the animal as he wheeled his mount and raced away.

That was when he discovered he had been hit, blood soaking through the left side of his ragged shirt.

6

More Visitors

McVittie had allowed him to keep his tobacco and matches and Selby now sat on the bunk edge, rolled a smoke and lit up. The deputy came down the passage and glared in at him. He was limping a little.

'You sure musta done that little gal wrong, mister,' he growled. 'Went to put my arm around her waist and she stomped my foot so bad I been hoppin' for a half-hour! Says no man ain't never gonna lay hands on her again!' He laughed, leering. 'It was the 'again' got me interested — you get all the way there sometime, did you?'

Selby glared through the smoke cloud. 'D'you think I'd tell you, Olsen?'

The deputy straightened out his face. 'I could make you, don't you never doubt that, you son of a bitch!'

'OK by me — open the door and we'll have at it right now.'

For a moment, Clay thought the deputy was going to do it. Then Olsen snorted. 'McVittie'd blow me in two, I done that. But I got ways of makin' you miserable till they waltz you to that cottonwood out there. We don't run to gallows but we got a good strong branch on that tree. Ropes've wore it almost through, but it'll hold long enough for you to choke.' He laughed again and spat through the bars. 'Pleasant dreams!'

Selby was annoyed with himself because he had let the stupid deputy get to him: he couldn't stop thinking about what the man had said. *It'll hold long enough for you to choke . . .* '

He had always thought it must be a lousy kind of death, hanging.

'Hell! After all this time!' he said aloud, crushing out his cigarette savagely against the stone wall. *Death by hanging* — and for something he didn't even do.

Not that that would matter to Guy Clutterbuck, or any of the others still alive. He knew Hannigan was: the man was now the powerful head of a mining syndicate that stretched across three states and, last he had heard, Tate Hannigan was aiming to become Senator Hannigan, representing Colorado. A man with plenty to lose if Clay Selby told what he had seen in that abandoned mine shaft all those years ago.

But who would believe him? Twelve years back, he had barely turned eighteen — now he was an accused murderer. Whose word would anyone take? His — or a man who could easily become the next Governor of Colorado?

But, of course, Hannigan couldn't risk it — Selby's claims, wild as they might seem, could still stir up some unwanted investigation by his political enemies.

Several times over the years Clay had had to abandon different new lives he had set up for himself, after his escape from Clutterbuck that night. The bullet wound in his side hadn't been too serious, although he lost a lot of blood and panicked some — after all, it was his first bullet wound. Since then he had lived through several more. Some delivered by killers sent after him and who had laboriously tracked him down. None ever said so right out, but he knew their pay packets came — by whatever devious means — from Tate Hannigan or Guy Clutterbuck. He couldn't believe it as the years went by — two, three, five, seven — that they still kept after him. Of course, they had even more to lose now than when he had witnessed the murder: what he knew could ruin them all, shatter the lives they had made for themselves.

Clay had heard on a couple of occasions that Rush Landers had sworn to kill him if it took him the rest of his life. Seemed when the gunfighter had been winged by Selby at the mine that night, the bullet had busted his gun arm, high up, and it had taken seven months to heal. Then the man had had to work on it for another six months before he regained anything like his old gunspeed. And he'd never quite made it.

But all wounds heal eventually — the most stubborn, of course, being those in a man's mind — and Landers had made himself a reputation as a gunslinger, a killer for hire. Top dollar could buy his gun — but word had reached Selby, using another name of course then, that Landers boasted that there was one chore he was willing to do for nothing.

Kill Clay Selby.

But Selby finally found a haven, down on the Border, switching back and forth to both sides of the Rio. He had become a tough man himself by then — of necessity — had a reasonable gunspeed that had been demonstrated on several occasions and he was still a crack shot with a rifle.

For the last five years he hadn't even heard of Landers or Clutterbuck, though he was always wary and on the lookout for strangers. As soon as a stranger hit a town where he was living and stayed over for a time without any obvious reason, he would quit, without explanation or warning. Ride out in the middle of the night and vanish, surfacing somewhere else many miles away under a new name.

Of course, he never tried to earn a dollar by the telegraph key: that would give him away too easily, but he had lived by a dirty dollar now and again, throwing a wide loop, a couple of times pulling a bandanna up over the lower half of his face and holding up a Wells Fargo depot, once a train — and that was a mighty heart-stopping deal. He never tried that again, having escaped only by a hair's breadth. That was how the drink-sodden sawbones in the backwater town had put it.

'The width of a hair of your stupid head, mister. Ye can tell your gran'children that's how close ye came to visitin' ol' Nick . . . the bullet actually brushed your black heart before burstin' out of your back!'

Too close for Selby. After recovery he got a job on an isolated ranch, gained experience in working cattle and breaking-in mustangs, and made the cattle industry his circuit, going from ranch to ranch, and, later, trail herd to trail herd, both sides of the Rio. He worked out of a base in Mexico where he had made many good friends.

He made several trail drives with Drag Stanton: they had hit it off pretty good, a bare ten years' difference in their ages, and Drag had become the closest thing to a trusted friend Selby had allowed himself in twelve years.

Though he had never told Drag — or anyone else for that matter — about his troubles, however hard they hinted they would like to help, for it was painfully obvious at times he was a man with a lot on his mind.

★ ★ ★

And now he was going to hang for Drag's murder — unless Clutterbuck sent someone to make sure of him and put a bullet in him first. Or even did it himself.

Guy Clutterbuck was high up in the United States Marshals' Service these days. He travelled a lot, working out of and running the important marshals' office in St Louis. Selby wondered if the 'travelling' was something he arranged for himself so he could keep searching for the kid who had out-gunned and out-smarted him that night all those years ago at Big Bear Rock. A man with the things on his conscience that Clutterbuck had, likely would never properly rest until he had seen Selby's body in a coffin.

And Cassie had damn well sent for him! Alerted the man to the fact that Selby was still alive!

But he couldn't blame her — He had simply disappeared from her life twelve years ago, no explanation, no contact since. She must have been terribly hurt and eventually that hurt had transformed into cold hatred. Many times he had been tempted to write but he figured her mail might be watched and he didn't want her involved.

They would know they could get to him through her — and — *hell!* — they could even *still* be watching her, hoping that one day she would lead them to him. Hannigan would certainly still see him as a danger. Clutterbuck, too, though like Landers, the marshal would likely be satisfied just to settle with him on account of that night back in New Mexico.

He groaned. What a mess! *What a goddamned mess!*

Well, he had to get out of here. That's all there was to it. *He had to break out — tonight!*

Only problem was, how the hell was he going to do it? One thing was for sure — he would have to make his try while that dumb deputy, Olsen, was still doing guard duty. If McVittie took over — well, he might just as well settle in and wait for the noose to tighten around his neck.

There would be no getting past that tough old Scot.

* * *

He need not have worried.

There were two men new in town, Johnson and Flail — later Selby thought they sounded like a vaudeville comedy team, though there was little laughter in the life these two led.

They were on Clutterbuck's payroll, and, after receiving Cassie Bier's wire more than a week earlier, the marshal had contacted these stand-by hired guns and sent them racing to Tucson.

Cassie wasn't yet in bed. Her visit to the jail and confronting Selby had been too upsetting. She relived those times of twelve years ago in her mind, feeling all the torment and emotion that had devastated her when it became obvious that Clay Selby had run out of her life and apparently would never return.

She went over imaginary scenes of what she would do or say if ever they met up again . . . And, of course, they *had* met up earlier tonight. She wasn't happy with the way her visit to the jail had turned out. She had had to work herself up to declare her hatred for him.

Right now, that hatred was boiling inside her because she had whipped it up from deep within, where it had almost — but not quite — been forgotten. She knew she would take hours to get to sleep and so picked up a book to read: it was one of Monsieur Dumas' swashbuckling tales of Revolutionary France and she had to concentrate on the meticulously detailed descriptions of practically every item seen by the heroine as her coach passed through the countryside . . .

The knock on the door surprised her — it was well after ten o'clock. She hoped it wasn't some drunken cowboy out on a spree — the town was noisy with the trail crew's celebrations which had followed hard on the heels of the wake they had held earlier for Drag Stanton.

She blinked at the two men standing in the lamplit passage. They were tolerably well dressed but their clothes had a layer of trail dust in places that had escaped whatever brushing down they had given themselves. They were polite, doffing their hats and nodding. The pale-haired one with almost white eyebrows spoke courteously.

'Sorry to disturb you so late, Miss Biers. My name is Johnson and this is Mr Flail. Marshal Clutterbuck sent us down to see you — you did send him a wire saying you knew the whereabouts of a wanted fugitive, didn't you?'

'Why — ye-es — I did.' She found herself stammmering a little, heart pounding. *Had she really wanted this to happen?*

'Good — then could you take us to him right away?'

'I — don't know . . . '

The darker one frowned. 'You said clearly enough in your wire you knew just where Selby was . . . '

Cassie looked from one to the other, seeing the hardness of their eyes and faces now, looking deeper than just the surface courtesy they displayed for her benefit.

And there were the tied-down guns, both notched . . .

'Well, I did at the time. But since then . . . ' — some deep instinct she was unable to ignore put unwanted words into her mouth — 'Well, he's moved on. He was with a trail herd and he . . . paid off — is that the term? — don't know where he is right now, I'm afraid.'

'We heard he might be in the local hoosegow,' the dark one said in that unfriendly voice. 'Accused of killing some Texas trail driver . . . '

She stiffened and allowed anger to show now. 'Then why bother me? Why don't you go straight to the jail and see for yourselves!'

The one with the pale eyebrows got his boot against the door before she could close it. He smiled without warmth. 'Because, sweetheart, we figured it'd be better if you came along and introduced us to the sheriff. He's a man with a tough reputation and might not like two strangers coming in at this time of night wanting to see his prisoner.'

Cassie's eyes narrowed. 'If Marshal Clutterbuck sent you, surely you have identification that would satisfy Sheriff McVittie as to your intentions?'

Johnson smiled thinly at Flail. 'Sounds like a real lady, don't she?' He reached suddenly, grabbed her arm and pushed her back into the room. Flail clapped a hand over her mouth before she could cry out, his other hand felt over her taut young body. She writhed, face reddening in fury.

'Just come along quietly, miss,' he told her, tightening his fingers over her mouth and pinching her nostrils. 'See how easy it'd be to knock you out . . . ?

And then we could have some real fun with a looker like you — but there's no need for rough stuff. You just take us down to the law office, introduce us to the sheriff as a couple of old friends of Selby's just passin' through and that's all.'

She didn't believe them but she was afraid of them, her heart pounding, shaking her small body. She walked between them down the stairs, across the dimly lit foyer, past the dozing night clerk and out of the hotel.

'Which way?' Johnson asked, and she pointed to her left.

Some of Drag's men were holding races on Main: men riding other men's shoulders like horses, even using their spurs, shouting and yippee-ing, egging the racers on, money changing hands as bets were laid. There was an occasional exuberant gunshot, and she wondered where McVittie was.

They skirted this racket and for a moment she was tempted to break free and run to the trail hands, calling for help, almost sure they would come to her aid, but Flail tightened his grip on her arm and murmured, 'Uh-uh!' in her ear. His teeth tugged at her lobe and she yelped, furious.

As it happened, McVittie had just looked in on Olsen to make sure everything was all right for the night. He stopped in his office and sat down at his desk to enter the time of his departure in his record book, figuring to put a stop to the shenanigans of the trail men on his way home. There had already been half-a-dozen complaints from citizens. He looked up irritably as Cassie walked in from the street.

'All right, lady, I know there's a lot of noise that needs tending to. Give me just a few more minutes and I'll . . . '

He stopped as the two men came in hard on Cassie's heels and Flail turned to close the street door. Old instincts kicked in instantly and McVittie stood abruptly, the movement knocking over his desk chair, as his hand drove down for his six-gun.

Johnson shot him in the chest, his gun sweeping up in a smooth blur, blasting, and continuing to rise briefly before the killer had control of the recoil.

'Damn you, Johnno!' said Flail bitterly, as Cassie stifled a scream, hands covering her mouth. 'I wanted to see if I could beat that old Limey! His rep's pretty good!'

'Was — I've had a hankering for years to see if he was as good as they say,' Johnson started, and then spun wildly as Cassie charged for the door, wrenched it open and ran out into the night. He lunged after her, but Olsen came rushing in from the jailhouse passage and Johnson lifted his gun again. But this time Flail did the shooting, two very fast shots, and Olsen slammed back through the passage door, slapped into the wall and fell on top of his unfired shotgun. His boots rapped the flagged floor in his death throes.

'The gal!' Flail yelled, but Johnson

was already starting down the passage to the cell block.

'Let's finish Selby first. Them drunks are too busy with their races to listen to anythin' she might say . . . '

Flail started after Johnson and they came to the cell where Clay Selby waited apprehensively, knowing instinctively what the shooting meant.

The gunmen stopped outside the door under the light of the lamp burning on the wall in its old rusted bracket.

'So — this is what's turned old Clutterbuck white-haired over the years,' said Johnson, shaking his head, looking at Selby who stood very tensely beside the bunk. 'Don't look like much to me.'

'They never do when they know they got less than a minute to live.' Flail lifted his gun and Johnson nodded, raising his own weapon.

'Yeah — get it done and clear town I guess while the drunks are still cutting-up. You ready?'

'Whenever you say . . . '

'I'm going for a belly shot — you?'

'Mmmm — little lower, I guess. Clutterbuck'll appreciate it if he knows the son of a bitch suffered while he was dying.'

'OK — now!'

Selby threw himself desperately under the bunk as he saw flame stab from the muzzles of the six-guns.

But he didn't hear the crack of the pistols.

The sound was blotted out by the thunderous roar of a shotgun — once — twice — and Johnson and Flail were picked up as if by some powerful wind. One man smashed into the bars and Selby, now on the floor, glimpsed a face that was nothing but tattered raw meat and gushing blood. The other man, Flail, bounced off the wall with a jarring grunt and fell sprawling on his back on the flagstones, blood washing from under his body which twitched and jerked.

7

Time to Go

Selby picked himself up, warily approached the bars.

'All right?' a voice called.

He released a long breath as footsteps approached down the passage. 'Danno . . . ?'

'And Mitch and Lacy,' Danno Magee said, appearing at the cell-door bars, still holding the smoking shotgun he had taken from Olsen's body. 'See they missed you — afraid I was too late usin' the Greener.'

Selby indicated a fresh splinter from the bunk frame and a long streak of grey lead across the rear wall. 'You timed it just right far as I'm concerned.'

Danno grinned and Mitch came forward trying to find the right key for the lock on the ring he had taken from the front office. 'Who were they?'

'Think they were a couple guns for hire called Johnson and Flail.'

Danno nodded. 'Hurry it up, Mitch — town might be OK with a few gunshots but a shotgun could bring some gawkers.' He glanced at Selby who was waiting impatiently for the door to open. 'We staged that drunken stuff out there — mostly not staged at all, just the boys with a snootful. Figured McVittie might drag a couple of us down to the cells where we'd've jumped him and got you out. But he let us go for a while and that threw us. Then we seen them hardcases half-draggin' that li'l gal, Cassie, along here and figured some-thin' was gonna happen — so we come a'runnin' — Jesus, Mitch! What's the hold-up — Ah.'

Lacy had shouldered Mitch aside, taken the keys, and within seconds had found the right one. The door swung open and Selby stepped out, jamming on his hat.

'You fellers are gonna be in trouble . . . '

'Who with?' asked Danno, leading the way. 'Olsen and McVittie are both dead. You run and you'll likely get blamed.'

'I'm running anyway!'

Selby glanced at McVittie's sprawled body in the front office, located his six-gun and belt in a desk drawer and buckled it on quickly. The man-horse races were still going and any curious townsfolk stayed indoors, peeking through their curtains.

'We've got your hoss around back,' Mitch said.

'Put in a couple extra boxes of ammo,' Lacy added.

'Thanks, fellers, but I'm not going right now.' They stared, Danno closing the law-office door and turning a key in the lock. 'Got to find Cassie. Where's she staying?'

'The Regal — least, that's where we saw her comin' out of with the hardcases. Clint — or Clay, whoever you are — you're pushin' your luck, man! We know you never killed Drag tho' damned if I know who did . . . '

He looked quizzically at Selby who said, 'Likely Johnson and Flail. Probably they jumped him, wanted to know where I was.'

'And he wouldn't tell 'em,' said Danno, nodding in slow agreement. 'So they killed him, come to town to find you. Must've looked good and easy to them once they found out you was in jail — for Drag's murder!'

'That'd be McVittie — a hard, suspicious son of a bitch, seein' crime where there ain't any,' commented Lacy. 'He's always been that way.'

'Not any more,' allowed Mitch. 'He had a bit of luck, though, with Drag's bad signature makin' it look worse for you, Clay. You really gonna take the gal along?'

Clay nodded. 'I've got this to do, Mitch — I ran out on her twelve years ago, can't do it again. Besides, she's in a lot of danger now.' He quickly shook hands all round. 'I'm beholden, fellers

— won't ever forget it. *Adios, amigos.*'

They watched him sprint down the street, cross over, amidst cheers of the drunken trailhands running yet another man-race, and saw him duck into the entrance to the Regal Hotel.

'Let's get back and keep the town entertained while he makes his move,' Danno said, and they hurried towards their drunken companions, Mitch holding up crossed fingers.

The night clerk jerked awake as Clay Selby slapped a hand flat on the counter, like a dull pistol shot. The man blinked, trying to orient himself.

'Miss Bier . . . which room? C'mon, man, I'm in a hurry!'

'Er — eight — But you can't . . . '

Whatever the man was going to tell Selby he couldn't do was lost in the clatter of Clay's boots as he sprinted up the stairs. He went left but soon discovered he should have gone to the right. A strip of orange light appeared as a door opened a crack and he glimpsed the figure '8' painted on the

120

panel. Then he saw Cassie's startled face and she began to close the door, but he pushed roughly with his shoulder. The force, although not really excessive, spilled her onto the floor and he stepped inside, closed the door behind him, leaning against it.

He reached down to help her up but she back-pedalled, eyes wide, shaking her head.

'St-stay away!'

'Can't. You're coming with me this time. Grab a few things. We've got to move!'

'I'm not going anywhere with you!' she gulped, but she wasn't fast enough to avoid his grip and he hauled her to her feet roughly, threw her onto the bed.

'Sorry, Cassie, you're in danger now. You saw those two men kill the sheriff and deputy — Clutterbuck can't let you live in case they trace those two back to him.'

She frowned. 'I — I heard a shotgun!'

'Yeah — Johnson and Flail're dead, but the man who sent them isn't.'

She frowned. 'They said Marshal Clutterbuck sent them, but that couldn't be right if they are — were — killers . . . '

'He sent them to kill me — can't go into it now. Time to go. C'mon.'

He shoved her protestingly towards the door, snatched up her small carpet bag from beside the bed, took her arm before she could run off and led her down the passage to the outside stairway. Danno Magee had said his horse was waiting behind the jail so he dragged her down an alley, lifted her, kicking and struggling, into the saddle of a cowhand's mount standing at a hitchrail. He swung up behind, dumping her bag in her lap, pinning her arms as he reached around her for the reins.

He rode down the alley and found his mount behind the jail where Danno had said. He transferred without dismounting properly, stepping deftly from one mount to the other, before she realized what was happening.

Then he grabbed her reins and spurred his horse forward, the girl's mount following automatically as it felt tension on the reins.

'Let me go! Damn you, Clay Selby! I — I'll jump off!'

He spurred again and his horse whinnied a little in protest but put on a burst of speed. The girl's horse followed and she snatched at the saddlehorn with a small cry.

In seconds they were travelling too fast for her to risk throwing herself out of the saddle and, faster than she would have thought possible, the sounds of the town faded quickly behind . . .

'Where are we — going?' she demanded, voice jerky with the movement of the horse.

'Far from here, that's all I know right now.'

'You — you turn me loose, Clay Selby! At once!'

'Jump if you want, but I'm not stopping for you.'

'You — I — I don't remember you being as bossy as this!'

'When you knew me, there weren't

123

people waiting to kill me — now shut up and hold on! We're going into the hills and it's rugged as all hell up there — we can talk later.' As the horse started up the steep slope, he bared his teeth in a mirthless grin and added, 'Maybe!'

Cassie held tightly to the saddlehorn, rocking violently as the horse hit the slope and bunched its shoulders for the long, hard climb.

* * *

It was almost two o'clock in the morning before Selby called a halt. By then Cassie was dozing in the saddle, tired beyond endurance. She had almost fallen a couple of times but he had dropped back alongside by then and steadied her.

Now they stopped on a rock ledge where several tall trees grew and behind these was an overhang of rocks that threw deep shadows, making it like an open cave. He helped her down and she sat on a fallen log while he made a small fire way back under the overhang, piling rocks around it to further hide its glow. She watched despite herself, still unable to think all that clearly, and then he thrust a mug of coffee and some hardtack into her hands.

'How did you know about this place? I thought you were a stranger to Arizona?'

'I am to this part of it, but I study maps covering the general area where I'm holing-up, talk to men who've been to places like this and tuck away the information in case I have to use it.'

She sipped the coffee, grimaced at its heat, and said quietly, 'You must live on your wits.'

'Guess you could call it that.'

'But — but whatever happened to drive you to this way of life? If that's what you call it!'

'It's the only way I've known for twelve years, Cassie, and I'm sure glad you weren't sharing it with me.'

She stiffened and he quickly held up a hand.

'I didn't mean it like that. All I meant was I'm glad you weren't exposed to the same danger I was, living on your nerves, just waiting to jump and move on — and hope it would be fast enough to stay ahead of a bullet.'

She frowned, studying him in that long and careful, searching way she had. 'I know you're Clay Selby, the boy I intended to marry, to *elope* with, but I don't *really* know you at all now, do I? You're an entirely different person to what you were in those days.'

'Twelve years have gone by, Cassie.'

'Yes — for me, too! I've suffered anguish most of that time, Clay, felt a hatred for you I'm not yet over . . . '

'I don't hold that against you, Cassie. You've a right to hate me and I savvy that . . . But there is an explanation. Do you want to hear it?'

He knew she did but could see in the dim, flickering light that the old stubbornness was still there and plenty active and she almost said no, she wasn't interested.

But maybe something about him reached down inside her and told her that here was a man who had been running for his life all this time — and that she had almost gotten him killed this very night because of her ignorance.

'I think it's time I listened to your explanation Clay,' she said quietly.

'Hope you're comfortable,' he said, as he rolled a cigarette and, when it was going, started talking.

He told her about the 'urgent' telegraph message that had to be delivered to The Drunken Lady mine.

'Hannigan was being warned by someone high up in the government, but he had already decided to get rid of his Mexican labour, anyway — and that was what I walked in on.'

She was horrified to hear his description of the twelve Mexicans being shot down in cold blood — and how the murderers had chased him and tried to kill him.

'They've been trying for twelve years

to make sure I never talk about what I saw, Cassie.'

'But surely — after all this time . . . Oh, of course, Tate Hannigan is very high in politics now, isn't he? He has a tremendous lot to lose . . . But, in all that time, why didn't you go to the law?'

'What did I have? Something I claimed to have seen, no proof, no other witnesses, and I was on the run. How could I hope anyone would take my word against that of a man who could be the next governor of Colorado?'

She nodded. 'Ye-es, I see that, but Marshal Clutterbuck puzzles me. He came to me not long after you disappeared, said I could get you to come in and he would do all he could to help you. I never did find out for sure what you were supposed to have done that made you run away — and that's been part of the trouble. *Not knowing!*'

She paused and he watched her fighting for control. Her emotions were barely beneath the surface, ready to break out at the least nudge.

'They claimed I tried to hold-up the mine office — the day before payday. That I assaulted the guard, wounded Rush Landers and another man as I made my escape. No one ever found the 'urgent wire' and they'd gotten to my records in the telegraph office, destroyed my copy and somehow shut the mouth of the other operator who'd sent it. It was the excuse they needed to keep after me, that was all. They didn't have to worry about ever making it stick because it was never intended to bring me in alive.'

She absorbed this while studying his face in the flickering light, watching the fleeting shadows darken and lighten his features. He was a man she didn't know: young Clay Selby had never had those hard lines, the coldness in the eyes, the jutting, aggressive jaw, or the alertness that clearly proclaimed here was a man ready to fight — and if he had to kill to resolve the current problem, then so be it . . .

That knowledge frightened her.

It had frightened her when those two killers, Johnson and Flail, had coldly shot McVittie and Olsen, and she had run, in fear of her own life. Only later, in her room and just before Selby had burst in, did she begin to realize that the men had come to kill him . . . McVittie and Olsen had merely been in the way and they had removed them cold-bloodedly. She expected them to come after her and, although she hadn't shown it, she was vastly relieved when Selby had come instead.

But she wasn't ready to forgive him just yet.

She had suffered her own torment all those years and it was only fair that he should know it. But it surprised her as she opened her mouth to berate him, to realize *that he already knew it!* And, what's more, he was genuinely contrite.

Impulsively, she reached out and closed a hand over his, bringing his flinty gaze around to her face. She felt the prickle of tears behind her eyes and wondered if he could see them glisten in this inadequate light.

Well, it didn't matter.

Because it was time she let him know he was forgiven — well, on the way to being forgiven: a girl had to keep a little pride, surely!

'I wonder if it might not've been better to leave me behind, Clay. I mean, those killers are dead now and — '

'Clutterbuck's not dead, nor is Hannigan — nor Rush Landers, far as I know,' he told her curtly. 'Nor are you, Cassie!'

Despite herself she sucked in a fast, noisy breath. 'You really think they would send people after me? Just because I contacted Clutterbuck to tell him I'd seen you and he sent those gunmen . . . ?'

Her voice trailed off and he knew she had realized that that was precisely why they would want her dead: because they expected Johnson and Flail to kill Selby and she would know who had paid them to do it. So *she had to die.*

He didn't tell her that they might not want her dead right away — that they would try to use her, in the hope that she would lead them to him once they knew he was still alive.

The danger was there whichever way you looked at it.

She wasn't aware of it, of course, but given time she probably would be. After all, she was an intelligent person.

Though bitter with a long hatred she really had no control over and even a genuine cause for feeling, now she was *really* involved.

He was debating whether to say anything right now or bring it out into the open a little later, when she stood abruptly, tossing away the dregs of the coffee, smiling faintly.

'You haven't learned to make very good coffee in twelve years — I'll have to teach you, I suppose.' She suddenly snapped her fingers. 'Well, don't just sit there! It's time to go!'

As he stood, she added softly, with a slow smile, 'Together.'

8

Call in the Favour

There was a man named Hart Brodie who ran a medium-sized cattle ranch in western New Mexico. He owed Selby a favour.

A *big* favour: Selby had saved the lives of Brodie and his wife, Karen, in a forest fire that had been deliberately lit by a neighbour who coveted their land. Clay Selby, using the name of Jim Brent at the time, had stayed on not only to help rebuild the fire-damaged ranch, but to give protection to the Brodies from the avaricious neighbour. The man, Spader, had brought in a gunfighter he figured would end it all and give him the spread.

Instead, it gave him a corpse to bury and when he personally tried to kill

Brent, had died himself from lead poisoning.

Hart Brodie swore right then and there that if ever there was anything — *anything at all* — that Brent needed, all he had to do was ask — any time, for the rest of his life.

Because he knew Brodie would go overboard if ever he did ask for help, Selby had never tried to collect on the debt. Not even when, some years back, he had been driven, penniless, hungry, afoot, with an empty water bottle and only eight cartridges for his rifle and six-gun, into the desert beyond the range, not far from Brodie's place.

He knew Brodie and Karen had wanted a family badly and he figured by now they might have children and he didn't aim to lead trouble to them. Somehow he had managed to shake Hannigan's killers once more that time, and he had not been in touch with Brodie since.

Now the years had gone by and *he* was in danger of losing *his* woman.

On their flight from Tucson, Selby and Cassie had made their way west in Arizona, out-running a bunch of hired gunmen when they followed the Colorado River north of Yuma, making for California. Cassie's mount had been shot from under her and she had hit her head badly in the fall. They rode double then, Clay holding her across his saddle, and were forced to make a desperate stand in some rocks. There was a long shoot-out and he was down to four cartridges when he killed three of the men, one after the other. Desperation often sharpens a man's eye — and trigger-finger. While the survivors scattered, Selby and Cassie had made their get-away. He gave up the idea of heading for California then: someone had obviously remembered he had often expressed a yearning to see the Golden State and put men on standby, waiting for him and Cassie to show up. It looked like they were still desperate to see Selby dead — and anyone who was with him at the time.

So Selby turned east and crossed Arizona, Cassie's health slightly improving, but she was still frail and a little vague at times, prone to fainting spells and double vision, the occasional terrifying nightmares.

He nursed her, bathing her after the sweat had drenched her body, washed her clothes in mountain streams.

She smiled wanly and touched his hand weakly. 'You can be so — gentle, Clay. I — I can hardly believe I've seen your face — blazing guns and — and bullets, and kill men . . . '

He grinned through the grime fouling his stubble. 'I wouldn't be so gentle if your name was Rush Landers or Guy Clutterbuck . . . ' He said it lightly, but the words wiped the smile from her face and her fevered eyes stared at him.

'I — I've brought this upon — you.'

'Hush, little Short Beer — I brought it upon myself a long time ago. I just wish you were somewhere safe, out of reach of these people.'

Then, one night after she had a bad turn and the screaming nightmares again, he thought of Hart Brodie and his ranch beside Coronado Creek, just over that purple-hazed range running at an oblique angle to the trail they had been following. There was help waiting — just over the range . . . if he could bring himself to ask for it.

And he knew that it *was* time to go call in that favour from so long ago.

Had to — if he hoped for any kind of a future for them both. And that was what he wanted now, more than anything else.

A future with Cassie.

★ ★ ★

'Jim! By God, it's Jim Brent!'

Hart Brodie came striding out of the barn, a dirtstiff leather apron covering most of his clothes, carrying a pair of fire tongs in one hand. He was a large man, younger than Selby, tow-headed and grinning. He dropped the tongs and began wiping his hands on a ball of cotton waste, reaching up to shake with the weary Selby. His grin disappeared as he saw Cassie, pale, bloodied, half-conscious. Then he brightened.

'Don't tell me that at long last you're in some kinda trouble I can help you with!'

Selby nodded and handed Cassie down to Brodie who steadied her gently, seeing the bad cut partly showing beneath the crude bandage around her head, and the bruise darkening that side of her face. Brodie clicked his tongue.

'Lord above! I'm sorry to be so happy about this occasion, Jim, but I've been waitin' — how long? Six, almost seven years to get a chance to square with you . . . '

'I wouldn't be here if I had any other place to go, Hart. This is Cassie. Let's get her inside . . . Karen there? With the kids?'

Brodie shook his head as, between them, they guided Cassie towards the house. 'No to both — seems we ain't meant to have kids of our own.' There was sadness there. 'Big house just for the two of us.'

It was the same log-and-riverstone building Selby remembered — his back still gave a twinge when he recalled how many buckboard-loads of river pebbles and rocks he had loaded and toted back here to set in cement.

'Karen's in town — gettin' some supplies. Our cornmeal order's delayed so she's stayin' over a couple days till it arrives. I don't mind, gives her a chance to catch up on gossip and have tea with her friends.'

By now, Brodie was directing them to a room at the back of the house on the eastern side. Clay carried Cassie in and she was grateful to stretch out on the bed.

'I'll go fetch Karen.' Brodie started to take off his leather apron. 'The crew's away, out on the range on a mustang drive. Only leaves my wrangler and the blacksmith here. They've both got jobs to do I'd rather not interrupt.'

'If you're real busy, Hart, I could ride in and get Karen?'

'Hey, Jim! There's no 'too busy' here. By Godfrey, don't you stop me now! Not after all this time. More bed linen in that closet. I'll get Cassie one of Karen's nightdresses — might be a little long but — anyway, you make yourself to home. And I *mean* that. Anything in the house, on the whole damn ranch, is yours, Jim. You just say what you want and if we've got it or I can get it, it's yours . . . '

Selby sighed as Hart Brodie dashed out of the room. Cassie looked up at him, her paleness tying a cold knot in his belly.

'This is why I've avoided coming here — I knew it'd be embarrassing.'

'He's so genuinely beholden to you, Clay, so eager to have the chance to repay you for whatever you did for him . . . don't spoil it for him now!'

He smiled, squeezed her shoulder. 'I

won't — we both need help. You with your injuries, me with a fresh horse, more ammo, supplies . . . '

'I heard that!' Brodie said, brightly, as he came in with a nightdress and robe for Cassie. 'You've got 'em all, Jim — or did I hear Cassie say 'Clay'?' Selby's face straightened and the rancher quickly held up a hand. 'Never mind! I knew before Jim Brent wasn't your real name but it's the only one I know you by so we'll stick with that. I'll get goin' now. I've told Renny, the wrangler, to look out for you till I get back. He's young but a real good feller . . . '

Selby was relieved to see Brodie ride out hell for leather a short time later. Already he was feeling embarrassed . . .

★ ★ ★

A few hours later, a rotund little man drove into the yard in a buckboard. He said he was Doctor Ballard and that Brodie had asked him to come look at

Cassie while he went in search of his wife.

'I thought he knew where Karen was,' Selby said, as the doctor started to unwrap the bandages around Cassie's head.

Ballard examined the wound and, without looking round, said, 'It seems Karen wasn't where he expected and to avoid delay in having someone look at your wife he asked me to stop by. I'm on my way to another of the outlying ranches.' He glanced up at Cassie. 'Nasty fall. Pupils are dilated still . . . you have double vision, my dear . . . ? Mmm, thought so . . . Nausea? Yes. Concussion, no doubt about it.'

'How bad, Doc?' Selby asked. He had seen cases of concussion that had eventually killed people.

'I believe she's over the worst of it — I'll leave some mild sedative and something to settle her stomach. Keep the light dim in here and it's bed rest, young lady, for a couple of days at least. Infusion of willowbark for the headache. You can see to that, I take it, Mr Brent?'

'I'll see to it, Doc — How much do I owe you?'

'Nothing — Hart is meeting all costs. Now, it's no use complaining to me! He's left me some money in advance. If the arrangement's not to your liking, then you'll have to take it up with him . . . I'm already running late . . . '

The doctor left ten minutes later and Selby gave Cassie a measured dose of each of the medicines, closed the drapes and told Cassie to get into the nightgown and then go to sleep.

She protested but the exhaustion of the past few days and the sedative combined to overcome her objections.

Clay closed the door quietly and went out onto the porch to await Brodie's return.

★　★　★

143

He was still waiting thirty-six hours later.

'This normal?' Selby asked the wrangler, walking down to the corrals to speak with the man.

Renny kept stalking the horse he was ready to break-in, didn't take his eyes off the animal as they circled each other warily around the corral with the firmly set snubbing post in the middle.

'Sometimes the boss decides to stay over with the missus.' He tossed the rope, snared the horse and was dragged, sliding upright, around the corral. 'Not unusual!'

Not likely in this case, though, thought Selby. Unless — unless because he had sent out a doctor, Hart Brodie had decided he could spend some time in town with Karen . . . ?

No. It didn't add up, not from what Selby knew about Brodie. He walked back slowly to the house. Cassie had been sleeping a lot since she had started the medicine and was looking better, had more colour in her face, but still

144

seemed quite weak and a little vague at times. Maybe it was the sedative itself that was making her like this. Anyway, the bottle was almost finished.

He looked in on her and she was sleeping soundly and comfortably. It was mid-morning and still no sign of Brodie or Karen.

It didn't sit easy with Selby. His guns were fully loaded now, as was his bullet belt, and he had a spare box of shells on hand. Brodie had left a grubsack full of supplies with filled water canteens, in case Selby had to leave in a hurry.

'But I sure hope not,' he'd added. 'I ain't finished what I want to do for you yet by a long ways. You'll be still here when I get back with Karen and soon as Cassie's feelin' better, we'll have us a little reunion . . . Man, you dunno how long I've looked forward to that! Be back quick as I can . . . '

And here it was, going on towards two full days now and still no sign of him. Selby knew Coronado Creek township was only a fifteen-mile ride.

He couldn't shake the uneasy feeling that something unexpected had happened — to Karen, or Brodie himself. *Or both!*

He didn't want to leave Cassie, although both Renny and the other cowhand who doubled as cook, name of Yankee Bill, were good enough men. He felt he could trust them but was reluctant to put them to the test.

Maybe he was being stupid, worrying unnecessarily, but he couldn't shake the feeling that something was wrong.

Badly wrong.

Then, just before sundown, Hart Brodie rode in and Clay Selby knew his fears had been fully justified.

Brodie could barely sit the saddle, he had been beaten so badly.

★   ★   ★

They got him inside between the three of them, Renny, Yankee Bill and Selby.

They put him on the sofa in the lounge and Renny, obviously familiar

146

with the house, went to a cupboard and brought back a bottle of whiskey and a shotglass. He poured it full and held it against the swollen, cut lips of his boss.

Brodie hissed and jumped as the raw spirit stung the deep cuts. Then he steadied Renny's hand with both his — and Selby noticed the knuckles were skinned and bruised; so at least Brodie had put up a fight of some kind. Gasping, the rancher nodded to Renny for another drink and gulped this down, too, coughing this time.

One eye was half-closed. His cheekbones were both swollen and bruised, his jaw looked lopsided and his nose was a squashed mess: his good looks would suffer from this hammering, Clay thought. His shirt was ripped and raw. Scraped skin showed through the rents, also bruising, as if he had been kicked.

There was a goose-egg knot on his head and a little blood matted his tow hair. He blinked away stinging tears caused by the whiskey and coughing, managed control and looked up at Selby.

'S-sorry, Jim.' His voice was hoarse, raspy, the words barely understandable.

'Don't strain, Hart,' Selby told him. 'Take your time — Bill, is there any coffee?'

Yankee Bill slipped away to the kitchen and Brodie tried to clear his throat. He took the cup of coffee between both scarred hands, sipped, and grimaced, but made himself take a couple of swallows. He sighed.

'Feels better,' he said, voice clearer now and swivelling his gaze to Selby. 'You know — somebody named — Rush Landers?'

Selby stiffened, all eyes on him now.

He didn't have to speak: his answer was clear to see by his reaction.

'Well, he's in town,' continued Brodie, his voice beginning to tremble now. 'And he's got my Karen! And he says he'll kill her if you don't meet him at a place I'll tell you about by ten o'clock tomorrow morning!'

9

Rendezvous

From Rush Landers' point of view, he must have figured he had chosen the rendezvous well.

And he had — if he wanted to set a trap for Clay Selby. It was obvious that this was what he had in mind. Clay saw it at once, when Brodie led him through the timber and stopped on a narrow ledge pointing down. It was still barely daylight but Selby could see what Brodie was indicating silently, moving his arm back and forth.

'Yeah — four perfect places to set up bushwhackers,' Clay said quietly.

'That broken rock in the middle with the brush skirt around it is where he wants you to stand . . . a crossfire will turn you into a sieve in about ten seconds.'

Brodie's voice was tight, clipped. He was stiff and bruised from his beating, but had insisted on coming with Selby.

They had left the ranch well before sun-up and Hart Brodie had led the way in, staying away from the normal trail to town in case Landers had men watching. He had told Selby that when he had ridden into Coronado Creek and didn't find Karen at the hotel where he expected, nor at two of her friends' places — they had told him she was to meet them for lunch but hadn't shown up and they didn't know where she was — Brodie had felt the first misgivings.

But being the kind of man he was, he looked up Doc Ballard and sent him out to visit Cassie at the ranch before starting his search for his wife. He scoured the town without success and was considering going to the sheriff, but learned the lawman was on his way to Albuquerque, answering a summons from a Federal Marshal. (Later, this would be found to be a fake message, simply to get the sheriff out of town.)

Stomach wrenching, he had stood outside the closed law office and built a cigarette with trembling fingers. Then a man he knew as Windy Gale, a loafer who hung around the saloons, came up, doffing his hat. 'Howdy, Hart.'

'Windy, I'm in no mood for tall tales today — here's a quarter. Go get yourself a drink and enjoy it.'

The man grinned, showing gapped, dirty teeth. 'Why, thank ya kindly, Hart. But I — I got somethin' to tell ya.' He screwed up his face and, as Brodie lit up, suddenly brightened. 'Yah, I got it!' He spoke slowly as if examining every word to make sure he had it right before saying it out loud. 'Go to Mose Degan's ol' cabin off the Zuni trail — your wife's waitin' for ya.'

Brodie dropped the cigarette, stared at Windy, amazed at the message. The man seemed frightened then and went to turn away but Brodie grabbed him by his grimy vest and pulled him back sharply. 'Who told you that?'

Gale half lifted an arm, as if afraid Brodie might hit him: he knew the rancher was always a soft touch for a free drink and he had never seen him like this before — on the edge of a murderous rage . . .

'I dunno, Hart! Honest! Feller asked me if I knew you an' when I said I did, he gimme a silver half-dollar an' told me to find you and tell you what I told you — '

'You know the man, Windy?' Brodie asked, forcing himself to keep control. He didn't want to frighten the old bum into silence.

Windy hesitated, licked his lips, and nodded. 'But he'll kick my ass if he knows I told you.'

'Don't worry about that — who was it?'

'Lafe Dancey,' Windy murmured worriedly.

Brodie swore. Dancey was the local hardcase, did any kind of a job, mostly illegal, for a dirty dollar. His pastime was rolling drunken cowboys on pay day and he was a man who liked to sink the boot when a man was down and hurting.

'I went to Degan's place and this Rush Landers was there — with Karen,' Brodie had told the impatient Selby.

'She all right?' Selby had asked, and Brodie nodded curtly.

'Mostly so — frightened, of course. Then without a word, two men I'd never seen before stepped out of the shadows and one hit me from behind. I went down to my knees and they beat the hell outa me, Jim! Lousy, yeller bastards!'

Selby knew Hart Brodie was not a man given to swearing so it had to have been humiliating for the rancher as well as mighty painful.

'Karen was hysterical by this time but they gagged her and threw her on a bunk and tied her hands and feet. Then Landers squatted in front of me and said, 'What happened to you can easily happen to your wife, Brodie — or worse. All you gotta do is ride back to your spread and tell Selby to meet me at Jackass Rock by ten tomorrow mornin' — then you an' your wife can go.'' Landers, face sun-dark and heavily lined with vertical creases running either side of his cruel mouth, had smiled thinly, adding, ''If he don't show, we'll kill your woman — but not right away, you get my meanin' . . . ?''

'He'll kill you both, Hart,' Selby had said. 'Sorry about this. How the hell did he know I was at your place?'

'Said your woman was spotted leavin' the stage swing-station this side of Fort Apache and they figured you were headin' for my place. They knew you'd worked for me once. You can see why he chose this spot as a rendezvous.'

Selby nodded slightly. 'We picked up some fresh mounts at the swing-station. Damn!' There was no doubt in Clay's mind what Landers intended to do. Then a thought struck him as he studied the layout from up on the ledge and he glanced at the battered Brodie.

154

'How was Landers? Got a stiff arm, maybe?'

There was a sharpness in the look Hart gave back to Selby. 'Right arm seems kinda — I dunno. It sort of *jerks* when he moves it instead of goin' smoothly.'

Selby nodded. 'I winged him twelve years ago. I heard he'd had trouble with his gun arm but was overcoming it. Seems he hasn't beat it yet. That's why he aims to set me up for bushwhack. Claims I ruined his reputation as a fast gun — and he meant the *fastest* if I recollect right. He'll make sure of me by having a man or two planted around the rock down there . . . which is why I wanted to leave so early. Get here before the killers move into position.'

'Jim, I want Karen rescued. I'll pay any price — *any* — price to get her out unharmed. I know how much I owe you, but there's a — a limit to my commitment to you now. You have to understand that — I'm sorry but . . . '

Selby raised a hand. 'No apology,

Hart — I had no right coming here in the first place. No! I mean it, no right. I just didn't think these sons of bitches still wanted my scalp so bad, or that they could get organized again so fast. I see now that they've been ready to go for all those years.'

Brodie's bruised and swollen jaw dropped a little. 'You mean — *twelve years*, they've just been waitin' for you to show again? Judas Priest, Jim! What in blazes do you know about 'em?'

'Hart, the less you know the better. It's just that the men involved twelve years ago have a helluva lot more to lose now. None of 'em can rest easy until they see me buried under a headstone. Or a couple of tons of rock.'

Brodie was still puzzled and amazed. 'By God, Jim. I dunno as I would've — no! Damnit, that ain't right! You saved my life and Karen's and I *owe* you, no matter what. But, like I said, there are limits to how far I'll go.'

'Understood, Hart. You didn't have

to come now. In fact, I can handle this if — '

'*If* nothin'! I'm gonna help, but I gotta tell you, Jim, if I see a chance to break off and get Karen away safely, I'm takin' it. I — I'll have to!'

Their gazes locked and Selby nodded gently. 'Relax, Hart — I savvy, really. Just don't take any risks. You watch for that chance to break away and get to Karen — I'll handle these other varmints. What'd the two men who beat you up at Degan's hut look like?'

'One's kinda of like — like a beer barrel, I guess, just about as wide as he's tall. Has a black beard but I think it's mainly to — '

'Hide a scar on his left cheek, that runs like a streak of lightning up beside his eye,' cut in Selby, and when Brodie nodded, he added, 'Cat Sheldon — s'posed to be a back-shooter and I believe it. The other wouldn't be about my size, hair drawn back behind his head in a tail tied with a beadwork buck-skin band, would he?'

'That's him. Think Landers called him Simm.'

'Simm Saul, another one with bloody hands. They were mixed up in what I saw twelve years back. Looks like they haven't progressed much, but that don't make 'em any the less dangerous . . . And this Mose Degan, what's he like?'

'Ought to fit in well with Landers' bunch, I reckon. Drinker, some say he brings in Mexes, and when they're no more use instead of payin' 'em in gold, he does it in lead.'

Clay nodded grimly. 'Oh, yeah, he'd be right at home with Landers' bunch — and the men they work for. All right, we've got to figure that Landers is gonna use all these fine upstanding citizens down there.' He nodded towards the basin surrounding Jackass Rock. 'You pick out what you reckon'd be the best spots for 'em to hole-up and see if they're the same as my choice.'

They were — places that afforded

good cover for the killers, and a good line on the target — Selby — who would be kept talking in just the right place by Rush Landers.

'But Landers'll want first crack at me,' Selby told the rancher, who was dabbing at his nostrils which had started bleeding again. 'The others are there for back-up.'

'What am I s'posed to do? I can't watch all of 'em at once, Jim!'

'Maybe you won't have to. Landers'll likely leave a man out along the trail watching for me — and unless I miss my guess, the other two'll be in position long before ten o'clock.' He smiled crookedly. 'Might have to pay 'em a visit before Landers arrives.'

Brodie stiffened. 'Won't he want to check they're in position? Call out or something when he arrives?'

'Could be — in which case I'll just wave one of their hats or something.'

'But they'll be on opposite sides of the basin. What about the other one?'

Selby looked at him steadily. 'I need

one more favour, Hart.'

Brodie tensed. 'You want me to get rid of one and . . . wave his hat if I have to?'

'That's it, Hart. You're no killer, I know, and it's not easy to come up on an unsuspecting man and slip a knife in him or cut his throat . . . '

'Good God! I — I can't do that!'

'Won't need to. You could slug him with a hunk of wood, couldn't you? Or a rock? Think about Karen while you're doing it.'

Brodie was breathing hard now and his eyes were narrowed. 'I've seen you in a gunfight, Jim, and you're deadly, but I never thought of you as bein' cold-blooded. I mean, defendin' yourself is one thing, but deliberate murder . . . '

'Like I said, slug him hard. Karen's life, yours, Cassie's . . . and mine could depend on it.'

Brodie ran a tongue around his lips, nodded slowly. 'I'm not a fighting man, Jim. Unless I *have* to fight to protect my loved ones — and this is exactly that, isn't it?'

Selby agreed and they dismounted and ground-hitched the mounts out of sight from below and sat behind some bushes so they could watch the killing ground.

Clay Selby estimated it was about two hours till rendezvous time.

*   *   *

But the first killer showed up long before then.

Showed up and rode down into the basin quietly, rifle butt on his thigh, head turning this way and that, checking out the brush. It was Cat Sheldon and he scratched his beard as he looked around, laid his rifle across his legs and took out a cigarillo. He lit up — but didn't glance up at the ridge where Selby and Brodie lay. They were well hidden, but it seemed Sheldon didn't even consider that danger could come from above. He began wiping out his tracks lethargically and not well.

They watched in silence as he went about setting himself up by a deadfall just inside a line of screening brush. It was the first place Brodie and Selby had picked out as being a likely spot for a bushwhacker.

Before long, Cat Sheldon still relaxed and smoking, another cigarillo laying its scent on the morning, a second rider showed. It was Simm Saul, lanky, loose in the saddle, but with a short-barrelled shotgun across his thighs.

'You set, Cat?' he called.

'Yeah, I'm set, you dummy!' Sheldon replied hoarsely. 'You ain't s'posed to be callin' out!'

'Hell with you. Mose ain't comin' in yet, Rush has got him watchin' the trail for Selby.'

'Chris'sakes! Quit gabbin' and get in position! It's after nine-thirty!'

'Like I said — hell with you, Cat! *Miaowww!*'

Saul chuckled as he rode around the central rock and they could see the bushes waving as he made his way up the small blind gulch they had figured would be used. He made a deal of noise settling in, grunting, cussing, and apparently slapping his horse, because the animal gave a couple of startled whinnies.

Brodie, tight-faced, split knuckles white where they clenched his rifle, looked across at Selby. He licked his lips.

'You ready?' Clay jerked his head towards where Sheldon was holed-up, knowing how tensed the rancher was.

Brodie swallowed, nodded. 'I . . . guess.'

'Let's go . . . you be Ok?'

Brodie nodded again. 'I — I'll hit him with my gun butt.'

'Make it hard — he's got a head like granite.'

It should have gone off smoothly: neither gunman suspected Brodie or Selby were within spitting distance. They were early enough to fuss a little and make themselves comfortable, their preparations holding their attention as

Selby and Brodie sneaked up on them.

But Brodie in his nervousness slipped on an eroded rain trench and fell with a clatter, striking the brush and tumbling out into the open.

Selby, on his belly as he made his way around to where Simm Saul was in his blind gulch, swore softly, wrenched onto his back, bringing his rifle across his body. A shell was already in the breech and all he had to do to cock it was thumb back the hammer. Which he did — just as Cat Sheldon leapt to his feet and fired four rattling, rapid shots.

Gravel and dirt spouted around Brodie's still sliding body and he sprawled, his gun slipping from his grip. He made a motionless, easy target then, and Sheldon actually bared his teeth in a crooked smile that showed up against his black beard as he beaded-in deliberately.

Selby fired across his body, levered again, spun, sliding down the slope as he triggered once more. Cat Sheldon stiffened, started to turn — in time to take the second shot through the neck. Blood spurted in a fanning arc as he tumbled backwards — and by then, Saul was straddling a rock in his gulch and his shotgun roared its thunder.

Selby spilled into a hollow and a charge of whistling buckshot tore a pound or so of gravel and earth from the ridge cap just above him. He spat grit and launched himself bodily out of the hollow as Simm Saul triggered the second barrel.

The man was still standing, sure that Selby would huddle down in the groove. Which was exactly why Clay made his move out of the hollow in a desperate, headlong dive. Some of the buckshot caught his leather halfboot, kicked his leg violently and numbed it above his ankle. It twisted his body and he fell, floundering, but rose to his one knee, rifle to shoulder.

Saul was thumbing home his reloads, still hunched over, when Selby fired, once, twice, three times. Simm Saul's body was hammered by the lead, jerking as if caught by tugging wires. Selby started reloading the rifle as he ran back to where Brodie was now on his feet, blowing dust from the action of his six-gun.

'Sorry, Jim, it's that old ankle injury. Boot turned under me . . . '

'Get your horse!' Selby snapped, as he ran past. 'Landers must've heard that shooting. He won't show here now!'

'Oh, my God! And he'll have Karen with him!'

Clay Selby was well aware of that, and just how ruthless a frustrated Rush Landers could be.

They would be lucky to get her back alive.

Brodie probably knew it, too, but he said nothing. As they rode, Selby glanced at him now and again, saw the tight-set lips compressed into a razor-slash, the pale splotches beneath his bruises, the death-grip on the reins. Hart Brodie was suffering plenty, but he was determined to do his part.

Selby was wondering about Mose Degan — where was he?

They were a couple of miles now past the rendezvous and had cut Landers' trail almost a mile back in the direction of Jackass Rock. It was easy to see where he had reined up fast when he had heard the shooting, wheeled and started back towards the hills. He was leading another horse — its rider had to be Karen Brodie.

Selby turned his head to alert Brodie as a hunch hit him that Degan might well have been left along this trail in case the ambush failed.

That simple movement of turning his head saved his life. He didn't hear the rifle shot first — it was the crack of the bullet whipping air past his face. He might have imagined that he felt its slight scorch in passing, but the fact that it *did* pass was the most important thing. He dropped along the horse's neck and heard the rifle shots that followed the first. His horse lurched and propped stiff-legged. He slid from the saddle, and sprawled, rolling in the dust.

Selby glimpsed a man jumping excitedly atop a boulder, sighting in on him. Then Brodie's rifle cracked and Mose Degan reeled, started to fall. Selby came up to one knee, rifle whipping to his shoulder in a blur. Degan's body jerked and crashed into the boulder, sliding off awkwardly.

Selby's horse was mortally hit and he despatched it with a single shot, ran alongside Brodie's mount, holding the stirrup, to where Degan lay, gasping, a hand pushed into his bleeding chest. He slid his pain-filled eyes from Brodie to Selby. 'Rush . . . said . . . you were slipp'ry as a . . . snake.'

'Where's he headed?' Brodie snapped, and Selby knew the man was mightily worried about Karen. The rancher cocked his rifle and held it inches in front of Degan's forehead.

Mose Degan curled a lip. 'Who you . . . kiddin', Brodie? You ain't got the guts . . . '

168

Brodie went even paler, stiffened and the rifle wavered, began to lower. Selby started to speak, then jumped when the rifle went off and Degan screamed. Brodie had put a bullet through the man's foot. Looking sick, he levered in another shell and pointed the gun at the other foot.

'You wanta hear the question again?' Brodie's voice might have been trembling, but his hands and stare were steady enough — the latter cold and unrelenting.

Degan was sobbing, knowing he could die and take his information with him, but it would be mighty painful. He swallowed. 'Wait!' he yelled, in a choked voice. He flicked wild eyes towards Selby then back to Brodie. 'He — he's goin' to your — ranch. Says Selby's woman's there . . . '

'What the hell's he want with Cassie?' Selby said, but knew the answer as soon as he spoke.

'Why don't you go . . . find out?' gasped Degan.

Selby wanted to leave the wounded man but Brodie insisted on roughly bandaging Degan's wounds and leaving a canteen of water close to his hand.

'Why you doin' this . . . for me?' Degan asked, clearly puzzled.

Brodie didn't answer and by that time Selby had found the bushwhacker's mount and ridden it back, obviously impatient. 'Unless you know a short cut, we'll never get to your spread before Landers . . . '

Brodie shook his head slowly. 'There's no shortcut from here. A big ravine cuts right across the trail and we have to go round. There's no other way, Jim.'

Selby was already spurring Degan's horse away. He knew Landers had too big a start for them to overhaul him, but he had to try . . . after all, the gunman would have to skirt the ravine, too.

But Landers had one more trick up his sleeve to delay them.

When they crossed a small stream and entered thick timber, they came up over a slight rise, Selby leading. He hauled rein with a curse, deliberately tried to head off Hart Brodie.

But the rancher instinctively pulled rein, too, and Selby's horse slid past. Frowning, Brodie rowelled his sweating mount around the rear of Selby's and topped-out on the rise.

And wished he hadn't.

His wife Karen was hanging from the branch of a cottonwood with a piece of paper pinned to her blouse.

He could read it from there through the stinging tears that burned his eyes. Six words, scrawled in charcoal.

Come on, Selby! I'll be waiting!

10

Long Trail to Nowhere

Only Yankee Bill was still alive when they reached Brodie's spread sometime past high noon, clouds scudding, grey and swollen with the promise of rain.

Renny was sprawled in the corrals — which had been emptied of horses, and used, as Selby learned later to help cover Landers' trail. The wrangler had an empty rifle by one hand, brass shells scattered around his body. He'd been shot in the back of the head.

They found Yankee Bill in the kitchen but a trail of blood extended behind him down the passage where Bill had crawled to Cassie's room and back to the kitchen. The door was splintered and there were several bullet holes in the walls. Selby was grateful there was no blood inside, although some furniture was smashed and the bedclothes were strewn about wildly.

Brodie tended to Yankee Bill in the kitchen while Selby inspected the house, not expecting to find anything helpful. He returned to the kitchen and pushed Brodie aside as the man worked on the old cook. He snapped at Yankee Bill, 'He say anything? Leave a message?'

Brodie angrily thrust Selby away, surprising the man, glaring at him. 'Take it easy!'

Yankee Bill had two body wounds and one hand bullet-shattered. He was in a lot of pain, looked up at Selby with dulled eyes. 'He said — you'd know where to find him . . . '

'That all?' snapped Selby, and once again Brodie pushed him back.

'Go find your woman, Jim,' he said, in a strangely cold and dead-sounding voice. 'I've still mine to bury.'

They had brought in Karen's body wrapped in blankets and she now lay on the big double bed in the main bedroom. Selby felt his murderous anger drain from him as he stared at Hart Brodie's dejected figure.

'Hart, I dunno how to say just how goddamned sorry I am over this . . . '

'Take any fresh horse you can find still running around out there,' Brodie told him soberly, jerking a head towards the yard outside the window and ignoring the apology. 'Help yourself to grub and ammunition — then *ride out, Jim!* I — I don't want to see you ever again. I reckon I've squared my debt to you.'

'More than enough, Hart. Look, I'll lend a hand with Karen and — '

'No!' Selby actually winced at the savage set of the rancher's ashen face. 'You hardly knew her! She — she was going to name our first child after you, but — but the Good Lord didn't seem fit to bless us that way. No, Jim, or whatever your name is, just go. *For Chris'sakes go!* Before I'm tempted to — to shoot you where you stand!'

'Aw, Hart, don't blame him too much,' wheezed Yankee Bill. 'You never seen nothin' like that son of a bitch Landers when he come in here blazin' away. Only left me alive so's I could pass on his message to Jim . . . '

Ignoring Yankee Bill, Brodie said bleakly, 'I'll give you ten minutes, Jim, then I — I won't be responsible . . . '

Selby sighed, nodded, thrust out his right hand. 'I don't suppose you want to shake hands . . . '

Brodie turned away deliberately, set about finishing the dressing of Yankee Bill's wounds.

It was the wounded cook who called weakly, 'Luck, Jim . . . heaps of it!'

Selby rode out in about eight minutes, having roped a black stallion with a wicked eye that was wandering in the yard, filled his canteens and grubsacks and taken another carton of .44/.40 calibre ammunition. He didn't bother looking back.

He knew he had lost a good friend in Hart Brodie but didn't blame the rancher. Selby was the one who had used him and it had cost Brodie his woman.

That was something else to remember when he finally confronted Rush Landers.

★　★　★

He had puzzled for a time over Landers' message.

'He *said you'd know where to find him* . . . .' Yankee Bill had said and the first thing that hit Selby was that he *didn't* know where to find Landers. He had no idea — and he had felt the cold panic rising within him.

Hell! Was this another way of Landers turning the knife in the wound? Keep him guessing? Drive him frantic with false information — or no information at all?

He had trouble picking up a trail under all the trampled ground left by the horses Landers had driven out of the corrals. Most were scattered now around the range, though several were making their way back to the ranch yard like his black had done.

His heart had been hammering his ribs in accelerated effort ever since Degan had told him Landers was making for Brodie's place. The man had killed Karen and now taken Cassie hostage. What else would he do to make sure Selby suffered maximum anguish and pain? Was he hoping to drive Selby into making foolish mistakes, his worries about the woman overpowering good sense?

No. From what Clay had learned about Rush Landers over the years, the man was doing it for maximum cruelty — and he hated to think about trail's end where Cassie would be a major factor in the resolution of this long, long hate.

He couldn't think of where Landers might mean: *He'll know where to come* —

'Goddamn, I *don't* know where!' Selby shouted aloud, as he skirted the trampled horse tracks once more.

He made himself sit down on a boulder — sheltered from a bush-whacker's attack — and he took a drink of water from the canteen and rolled a cigarette. He smoked it way down to where the butt was burning his lips before tossing it away. And still he hadn't found a solution.

For twelve years, he had been hearing about Landers from time to time — the man had had a lot of gunfights, determined to prove he was the fastest. But Clay had worked out a long time ago that while Rush walked away from a lot of square-offs, none of the men he left dying in the dust had been real top guns. He figured then that the man's arm had never fully recovered from that hasty shot he had fired at The Drunken Lady that fateful night. Which meant that Landers hadn't reached his goal of being known as the fastest gun alive. Even then he had known that Landers would keep after him and wouldn't rest until he saw Selby's corpse lying at his feet with his lead in him.

But he had managed to hide his trail well for a lot of years now — yet Landers had been there almost immediately he had been inadvertently betrayed by Cassie Bier. She had wired Clutterbuck, who, as far as Selby knew, was still working out of the important federal marshal's office in St Louis. Certainly her wire must have reached him — but that didn't necessarily mean that Guy Clutterbuck was still working in St Louis. If he had retired, any messages or mail would be forwarded to him as a matter of courtesy. He might even have left a request for that.

What Selby was trying to get at in his mind was: where would Clutterbuck go if he had left the Marshals' Service?

The man must have plenty of contacts below the Rio because he had been the one to organize the illegals for Hannigan's mine — and no doubt other ranchers who wanted cheap labour. But Selby, over the years, had never heard of Clutterbuck spending much time south of the Rio. He guessed the negotiations were long established and carried out by trusted couriers or even the mail service.

Then he remembered! A couple of years ago . . .

Drag Stanton had been running a deadline, getting a herd together that meant a high profit, but he was short-handed because it was late in the season and all the trail hands already had jobs. Danno Magee had told him about an agent he knew who could get a handful of illegal *vaqueros* to help out for the right amount of dollars. Small-time, but . . . . Drag had been just desperate enough to give him the OK to deal with the agent, but it had never happened — *because the agent had had a better offer, working as a recruiter for some sort of mine syndicate in New Mexico!*

At the time, Selby had made certain he showed no reaction to this — and had thought afterwards that it would be too much of a coincidence for it to be The Drunken Lady syndicate. Later, he had introduced the subject of illegal labour into the conversation when he had been riding with Danno on the northside wing of the trail herd just before crossing the Pecos.

Magee hadn't known who the agent had gone to work for, only that he was now headquartered in Albuquerque . . . and growing rich. It seemed a permanent set-up because the man had even got himself married.

Maybe it was grasping at straws, but Selby had no other chance, he figured. He found his way into Coronado Creek from the south trail and went straight to the telegraph office. It was late afternoon and it was raining heavily — which meant any tracks left by Landers would be washed out, anyway. The sour operator was thinking about closing down for the day but sent Selby's wire to Danno in El Paso with bad grace. It was brief:

Name of your friend in Albuquerque.
Moved from El Paso two years ago.
Urgent. Clinton.

'Urgent or not, friend, you ain't gonna get a reply tonight, because now I've sent this, I'm closin' up.'

The telegraph operator was a dour man with thinning hair, looked henpecked, but might have just been harassed from overwork. Selby offered one of his last two cigarillos to the operator who reached for it, but hesitated, and looked levelly at Selby.

'This won't get me to stay open.'

Selby shrugged. 'That's OK, — I've been in the same position when I worked a telegraph office.'

The man showed interest as he scraped a match alight on his desk and lit his own and Selby's cigarillo. 'Yeah? Where was that?'

'Patchett, New Mexico — ten years or more back.'

'Hell, my father-in-law ran that dump for a long time.'

'Get away! Not Fingers Finn by any chance?'

'None other! Hell, you know, he taught me how to use a key — met my wife through him — which he weren't keen on — knew a telegraph man din' make much . . . Well, well. You musta been a trainee back then?'

Selby said he was and they reminisced and time passed and the operator broke out a bottle of whiskey and Selby offered to buy supper.

'Buy, nothin'! You come home and meet the wife. She'll be tickled pink that ol' Fingers trained you . . . '

It was a good evening and when Selby was taking his leave, he thanked the woman and said casually to the man, 'I don't s'pose you'd open up long enough for me to check if there's a reply to my wire, Asa?' On a first-name basis now.

Asa's face straightened and his eyes narrowed, wondering if he had been flimflammed, but he had enjoyed the evening, too, and, with a little urging from his wife, agreed to open up the telegraph shack.

'Just to see if anythin's come through . . . '

There were three sheets on the repeater, the middle one the reply Selby was looking for.

Trace Kennett. Likes cards and women. Dangerous. Will come if you want. Danno.

'Thanks, Asa.' Selby took his last double eagle from his pocket and slid it across the desk. 'It was a good night — I liked your wife.' He grinned. 'She's better-looking than her father as I recall.'

Asa wasn't too graceful about accepting the money but he finally took it, then hustled Selby out and locked up behind him. The rain had stopped but the night was still damp and the air was thick.

'I've heard of this Kennett, too — miserable son of a bitch, quick with a gun.'

Selby nodded, sighing. 'Just what I

need, Asa, but thanks again, *amigo*.' He proffered his hand but was ignored.

'You never knew Fingers, did you? It was all lies what you said about him over my supper-table.'

Selby said slowly, 'No, not lies. He'd left just before I got there. My teacher was Carl Cannon — big admirer of Finn. He told me dozens of stories about him, which is what I spoke of tonight. I'd like to've known him, Asa. The man's a legend.'

'If ever you come back this way, just keep goin', OK? There'll be no more free meals.'

As Selby rode out of town with the wet wind ballooning his torn poncho about him, he figured he might end up with some kind of complex, if people kept telling him they didn't want him in their lives . . .

★　★　★

He timed it to hit Albuquerque just after sundown.

Most buildings were old Spanish-Mexican style with flat roofs and cut a low silhouette against the brassy blaze of the setting sun. Lights were burning on the walks and in houses and places of business around the central plaza. There were three cantinas and he housed the black in the livery, telling the hostler just to give him a nosebag of oats.

'Can throw in a currry-combin' and some grain and straw,' the man said hopefully. 'All one price.'

'Just the nosebag,' Selby repeated wearily and the hostler shrugged, but Clay gave him the full dollar anyway. 'Have a beer on me, *amigo*.' His money had dwindled to a handful of silver and a couple of bills. It might be enough.

And if he had to quit town in a hurry, it would be easier to rip a nosebag off the black and hit leather at a run than letting the mount bloat itself on grain, relaxing after a grooming.

He hefted his rifle, decided to take it with him and checked out the cantinas.

No one seemed very friendly once he mentioned Trace Kennett's name. But he found the man in the third and last cantina, half-screened by a cloud of smoke at a baize-covered table in a rear corner of the bar room. Five players were seated around the table with him.

The rifle got a few wary looks as he ordered a whiskey at the bar, tossed it down, asked for a beer, and took a big gulp to soothe his scorched throat. Holding the beer glass in one hand, the rifle in the other, he sauntered over to the table and leaned against the wall, watching the game.

A couple of the players frowned as he propped the rifle beside him but he just nodded in friendly manner. Trace Kennett was a well-groomed, well-fed man in his early forties, smiling with white teeth around a half-smoked cigar, as he dealt cards to the players.

'And two for the dealer,' he said, flipping two pasteboards onto the table in front of him. He separated his five cards, tossing two onto the discard pile, sorted out the new hand and made his face carefully blank.

Clay pursed his lips. It could be that he had a full house or a straight or a flush and was trying to hide his elation from the others — or it could be a smart player's move, letting the others see him deliberately compose his face so they would *think* he had a winning hand and was trying to cover up.

In one of the other cantinas, Clay Selby had spent most of his remaining money buying a few beers for some locals who had said they knew Kennett — that the man played only at the Chiquita, the third cantina on the plaza. He had learned that Kennett played for big stakes, had been accused of cheating a few times — and killed or wounded the men who had made the accusations. Others were leery and often were too afraid to speak up, tossed in their hands and quit the game.

All in all, Trace Kennett was disliked, but rich and powerful enough to get more or less what he wanted.

Selby watched the faces of the players as they placed their bets, saw the wariness in both the size of the bets and the demeanour of the men. He saw the tension, too, when Kennett scowled and glared around the table.

'You damn pikers! Make the game interesting, for Chris'sakes! You think I want to waste my time night after night on penny-ante stakes? *Come on!*' He slapped a well manicured hand down flat on the table making the cards and glasses — and the players — jump. 'Poker's s'posed to be a man's game. Well, I'm playin' with a lot of namby-pambies still wet behind the ears tonight! Let's see some real money in the pot! *Now!*'

He could bully them all right, Selby allowed silently, as he watched the men hurriedly get out wallets or dig in pockets for some gold coins. Then Kennett said they would leave the pot as it stood, but start another round of betting so as to build it up into something worthwhile.

'That ain't in any poker game I've ever played,' allowed Selby suddenly, and activity at the table froze. A couple of the men licked their lips, hands poised in mid-air over the pile.

Trace Kennett looked up slowly, arrogantly, light gleaming off the pomade on his wavy hair. He narrowed his eyes as he took in Selby's figure. 'Who the hell're you?' he demanded.

'Just an onlooker . . . '

'Then . . . shut . . . your . . . mouth!' snapped Kennett, and some of the players started to hurriedly push back their chairs but stopped at a snapping wave of Kennett's hand. 'Stay put! We'll get on with the game soon's I take care of this nosy son of a bitch!' He stopped abruptly and his eyebrows shot up. 'Well, well, well — you're him, aren't you? You're Selby.'

All the players were white-faced now and a wave of silence rolled across the room. The barkeep stopped, casually reached below the counter and closed his hand over a sawn-off shotgun — ready for whatever happened next.

The tableau at the table hadn't moved since Kennett's insult.

'Expecting me?' Selby asked casually, still relaxed against the wall.

'Rush said you might be along.'

That sent a tingle through Clay. *So he was on the right trail.*

'I'm here — and I want your help, Kennett.'

'I'll help you into hell!'

Maybe Kennett had been expecting Selby to go for his rifle, for he was caught flat-footed, reaching under his well-cut coat for the pearl-handled Smith & Wesson. 38 pistol he carried.

Selby's six-gun swept up and the barrel stopped about two inches in front of Kennett's suddenly bloodless face, hammer already cocked. '*No!*' the man gasped, the word barely audible.

There was an audible double *click*! and Clay knew it was a shotgun cocking. He whirled, gun rising: he ought to have known that a man like

Kennett would have back-up. Running an illegal labour business, he likely had the local law in his pocket, too. No time for theories, he realized, as he saw the barkeep lifting his weapon.

Selby upended the table into Kennett, dived left as the shotgun thundered and blasted a hefty bite out of the card table, pasteboards and money flying in all directions. Men ran for cover as Selby rolled up to one knee, chopped at the Colt's hammer with the edge of his left hand. It bucked and roared, a hail of bullets shattering the bar mirror, one catching the 'keep in the shoulder and sending him crashing into a shelf. He fell, legs going out from under him, bottles raining down upon him as he sobbed, shattered bone showing.

Kennett was crabbing away now, his Smith & Wesson in his hand, still very pale. Selby ducked as the man fired, put his last shot into Trace Kennett's side. The man went down, moaning, dropping his gun. Staying low, Selby crabbed his way across, got in behind the shattered table. He snatched the Winchester up, levering, swept it around the room, but no one wanted to buy in.

Kennett was still crying with pain, clutching his bleeding side. He gritted to the second barkeep, 'Get me some towels, goddammnit! Someone send for a doctor!'

'Forget the sawbones,' Clay said, as a man made to dash for the batwings. 'You, barkeep, bring him a couple of towels. Then get on with your job. Me and Mr Kennett are gonna have a few words in private — got a room we can use?'

After the 'keep gave Kennett two towels and he started back around the bar to where his boss was moaning and holding his shoulder, the man indicated a door just beyond the reach of the oil lamps' glow.

Clay dragged the cursing Kennett to his feet and the man howled as he pushed him to the door, reached past him to open it, and shoved him roughly inside. It looked and smelt like a whore's room, but Clay and Kennett were the only occupants right now. Selby leaned against the door as Kennett dropped on the bed and fumbled to get the towel pressed against his bleeding side.

'Just tell me if Guy Clutterbuck still works out of the office in St Louis?'

Trace Kennett's voice was shaky and for a moment Clay thought he might throw up. Then he cleared his throat. 'You're behind the times — Clutterbuck quit the marshals three years back — retired to a ranch near Conchas Lake on the Canadian. He'd been buildin' it up for years . . . '

'From his Mex business?'

Kennett's eyes widened. 'Yeah, you'd know about that, wouldn't you? I took over from him, came up from El Paso.'

'Not interested in you, Kennett, just want to know how to find Clutterbuck's spread — and one more thing you can tell me: was the woman with Landers all right?'

Kennett looked sly, took his time answering.

'What woman?'

'The one he took hostage at Coronado Creek.' Clay's mouth was mighty dry and his belly was knotted like a hangman's noose.

Kennett shook his head. 'He was alone and goin' like the devil himself was after him. He never had no woman with him, mister, I'll swear that on a stack of Bibles.'

11

One Man's Hell

The words had frozen Selby. His thought process, his muscles, his instincts — all paralysed by those few casual words spoken by Trace Kennett.

He was alone — no woman with him.

And Kennett was prepared to swear to that 'on a stack of Bibles'. Not that Clay believed the man had any religious tendencies but the way Kennett said the phrase turned his stomach upside down and filled his body cavity with ice that settled around his heart.

God almighty! Had Landers given Cassie the same fate as had befallen Karen Brodie?

It didn't bear thinking about.

And he had no time to think about it anyway, because the door was suddenly kicked open and, without turning, Clay dived across the bed, past the startled, wounded man, and landed in the narrow space between the bed and the wall.

By that time, guns were roaring, the thunder deafening in the confined space, glass rattling in the window frame. The pane shattered and glass shards fell onto his shoulders as he reared up, rifle blazing. He glimpsed two hard-eyed men crowding into the room, both wearing tin stars on their vests. These would be the local lawmen — in Kennett's pay so as to keep the supply of Mexes flowing smoothly on the regular route up from the Rio.

Afterwards, he didn't recollect thinking these things consciously, but his brain knew them somehow. The rifle was hammering as he worked lever and trigger, using his left hand to hold down the barrel that wanted to kick up in recoil. Powdersmoke fogged the room. One man was down and writhing, the other gunman had slipped back into the saloon somewhere. The door was ragged with splintered wood.

Clay looked at the bed and saw Kennett sprawled across it — he would need more than a bar towel this time. He was lying on his back, one arm dangling, two fresh blood-spurting holes in his chest. Whether the wounds had been deliberate or an accident didn't matter now — least of all to Trace Kennett.

But Clay swore softly: now he wouldn't know if Kennett had been lying to him or not! And he didn't even have proper directions so he could find Clutterbuck's ranch.

Couldn't even be sure if that's where Rush Landers was headed anyway — alone or otherwise.

As he reared up, smashing the broken shards out of the window frame with the rifle barrel, he realized he had been wounded. Blood was running down his neck and when he touched his left ear he felt bloody, mangled flesh. Well, maybe it would improve his looks, he thought a little wildly, as he dived out into the night. Guns fired in the room again and he figured the second lawman had found some help.

He was in an alley, stumbled over crates and bottles and one empty keg, reached a lane that took him across vacant land to the back of the livery. Men were shouting behind him. A gun fired raggedly and someone cursed the man who did it.

In the livery, he glimpsed the hostler and started to bring up the rifle. But the man was holding Clay's black, saddled, a part-empty nosebag of oats hanging from the horn.

'Figured a man who only wanted a nosebag for a mount that looked like it'd travelled to Canada and back might need to leave in a hurry . . . ' The man winked. 'Besides, no one in this town's ever tipped me before. Luck, mister.'

Clay thanked him as he mounted, swung away and spurred through the big open doors into the corral area.

'Go left! *Left!*' the hostler called in a low voice.

Selby took the man at his word, found this direction took him around the corrals into open country past the town trash pile. There was a lot of shouting, fading fast now, and once a rifle opened up but he had no idea who was doing the shooting or who the man was aiming at.

It seemed only seconds before he cleared town and the whole night-clad country spread before him. He urged the big black on, holding a wadded kerchief over his bleeding ear, heading slightly north of east, hoping he was going in the general direction of Lake Conchas.

★   ★   ★

There was a posse.

Whether it came because Trace Kennett was still alive and had ordered it, or whether it had been one of the corrupt lawmen who survived, Clay

Selby never did know. Not that he really cared.

He was hounded and that only added to the sense of frustration and tension that had been with him ever since Kennett had told him Landers had come in alone.

He couldn't shake that shocking image of Karen Brodie dangling from the rope on the cottonwood, limp body twisting slowly in the gentle breeze. But one look at the contorted face, the eyes and the tongue, and you knew her death had been anything but gentle.

Then there was the torn clothing and the blood streaks on her legs showing through the ripped fabric . . .

He shook his head savagely — and felt his ear begin to ooze blood again. To hell with that — it was a minor problem. *He had to rid himself of those images of Karen — in his imagination he replaced her with Cassie — or he would go crazy!*

He resorted to deliberate anger. Letting it build, helping it along, thinking of every goddamn frustration and trouble and close shave he had endured since he had entered that mine so innocently with the 'urgent' wire — only to find that Hannigan had already anticipated it and was bent on mass murder. He flayed himself, made himself recall the old fears, the sheer terror of an 18-year-old greenhorn on the run from cold-blooded killers — and not knowing where to go or what to do . . .

What kind of life would he and Cassie be leading now if he hadn't taken that wire to the mine that night? No! Hell, quit that! Thinking like that would *really* send him loco.

But it worked. All that anger he had built up and mostly suppressed over twelve years came together, and he deliberately focused it on the posse pursuing him.

They were trying to stop him rescuing Cassie — and killing Landers, though that was secondary to the other.

He had to believe Cassie was still alive — *had to!*

So he rode into unknown country, reading the geography with an expertise he had gained over the years. The timber dipped and the vegetation became concentrated between the hills. There would be a canyon in there, with water, judging by the greenness and the way the sunlight flicked off glossy leaves. The sun was slanted now, rays beginning to show in approaching dusk, highlighting a ridge of notched clouds, touching them with molten blue-greys, a little gold, smears of peach and a deepening crimson down towards the horizon.

With luck, the posse would head for that canyon to rest up for the night. To make sure, he veered towards it, leaving tracks plain to see. Then he led the horse into the narrow stream and, as he surmised it had a rocky bed and, more importantly, a ledge of sandstone on the far, less-used side. The tracks of his mount were plain in the gravel on the approach side, but only wet blobs showed on the sandstone and the retained heat from the day's sun soon dried them. Afoot, he led the horse around as close as he could to the rock walls, but not allowing it to scrape and leave a sign. He made the entrance, veered back the same way as he had come, then found a trail with thick layers of leaves, mounted and made his way up to the rim.

The sun was a distorted, wavering fireball by now, molten gold, stretched out of shape and hazy with an envelope of dust. He rowelled hard, bringing a protest from the black, but it took off with hind legs unsnapping like a released spring. He cut across the face of the sun, hoping the posse wouldn't be able to make out his shape because of the distortion. The black crashed into heavy brush and he quit saddle fast now, for he had seen the posse's dust cloud coming down out of the bare-back ranges towards the flats. They would pick up his trail and by the time they reached the canyon, there would be slashes of heavy shadow and the cook-fires would be started . . . *he hoped!*

That's what happened. He counted seven men, some grumbling that they wanted to turn back, but the lawman he recognized from the cantina tongue-lashed them soundly and they turned in early, mumbling sullenly.

There was only one guard and he was one of the dissidents so settled down in a comfortable place and soon dozed off. Selby could have killed them all with one magazine-load from his Winchester. His simmering anger stopped at mass murder though and he worked back from the edge, lowering the rifle's hammer.

He didn't like killing good horses, which was his original plan, so he led his black down silently, patiently, from the rim, ground-hitched it in the brush. Its ears pricked up as it sensed the other animals in the canyon.

The fools had put all the horses,

mounts and pack animals, on a single picket line. He tapped the snoring guard with his Colt's butt to make sure he stayed asleep, cut one end of the line, knotted it and untied the other end. Then, the horses' reins still looped over the rope, he led them carefully around the sleeping posse, keeping to the thick layer of coarse sand. He almost made it, too, but two men stirred just as he was squeezing the mounts through the entrance and some of them whickered.

'Jace? What the hell you doin' with the mounts?'

'That ain't Jace! Too blamed tall!'

'Christ! It's Selby!'

The camp was in an uproar in seconds and Clay figured he had nothing to lose now, whipped the picket line through the rein ends and loosed three fast shots into the air, yelling and shouting.

The posse's mounts took off into the night and Selby ran for his black. There was shooting in the canyon now

— useless because he was well outside by this time. Just panic, and that was good, he figured.

He hit leather at the run, set the black after the running posse mounts and emptied the six-gun and fired four shots from the Winchester to make sure they kept going and scattered amongst the bareback hills. He cut out one pack mule and veered away towards the heavy timber.

The posse had one hell of a long, hungry walk back to town or, even if they were lucky and managed to catch one of their horses, it would be days before they got help out here and were organized again.

By that time, he hoped to have put a couple of bullets into Landers — and Clutterbuck, too, if he could get him in his sights.

* * *

Recovering the pack mule gave him a couple of advantages. He could take a long way round now that he had extra supplies, stay away from the more or less direct trail to Lake Conchas he was orginally going to take.

It, in turn, gave him the second advantage: any pursuers might think he wasn't headed for the lake at all. But there was the risk that they could figure he was only taking the long way round so as to confuse or even shake them. In which case they would come hell-for-leather, or split up, half following him, the other half making post-haste for Clutterbuck's spread on the Canadian.

Still Selby could keep going longer each day now that he wouldn't need to hunt his grub. There was plenty of food in the mule's packs, some ammunition, too, and a half-box of dynamite complete with fuse and detonators.

That was a third advantage he hadn't discovered until his first stop after leaving the posse stranded in the canyon. *He might find a use for those explosives* . . .

Clay's theorizing was accurate enough — except for one thing.

After a posseman had managed to recapture one of the horses, the lawman hauled him out of the saddle, ordered the others to keep trying to trap more of the mounts while he rode back to Albuquerque. He didn't say why he was going, but although he arrived just before midnight, he pounded on the door of the telegraph shack until the sleepy, angry operator opened up and asked in slurred tones just what the *hell* was going on?

'Get dressed!' snapped the lawman. 'I need to send an urgent telegraph!'

'The hell with that! My workin' hours end at sundown! I don't rate no night-time relief in this lousy town!'

The man reared back as the law-man's gun muzzle pressed against his cheek and the hammer ratcheted back loudly.

'You just become civic-minded, friend, and you're gonna donate some of your time to *sendin' a goddamn*

telegraph message for me!'
The operator was persuaded.

★　★　★

Clay Selby knew nothing about the wire the lawman had sent, but he walked right into the results of it after he crossed the Canadian River just south of the lake to the small town of Pueblo Chico. It was too small to employ a lawman but he asked in the general store if anyone knew the way to the Clutterbuck spread.

The man behind the counter in the dry goods section was just rolling up a bolt of calico and looked sharply at the dusty stranger. He ran his gaze up and down and didn't seem unduly impressed with what he saw.

'Another gunman, I s'pose,' he murmured, just loud enough for Selby to hear, but low enough so that if there was a hostile response the storekeeper could claim he said something entirely different.

The only response he got was a hard look from Selby, but patient and uncompromising. The man cleared his throat.

'You — you're on the right side of the river. South about ten miles you'll see the sign at the fork in the trail. Er — you need any supplies?'

'No, thanks, *amigo*. Got all the bullets I need.'

The storekeeper smiled wryly as Clay left, nodding to himself: he knew he had picked him right — just another gunnie come to join Clutterbuck's hardcase crew . . .

Not quite, mister — not quite!

But Clay Selby almost *did* join the gunslingers of Block C.

Not as a new recruit, though.

If he hadn't curbed his impatience, forced himself to scout around first, he would have ridden into an ambush that would have left him bleeding from more holes than you'd find in a block of Swiss cheese.

And he didn't like the odds — from

what he had seen from his hidden observation point high in the boulder pile halfway up Conchas Mountain, he figured the odds at least ten to one — in Clutterbuck's favour.

He had arrived, all right, but what the hell was he going to do now?

One man against ten gunslingers he could see — and God knew how many others were waiting at Clutterbuck's ranch house.

And the big question: was Cassie even in there? Or was she somewhere along the back trail, swinging at the end of a rope tossed over a low-hanging branch in some dark and lonely place where even the buzzards would have trouble finding her?

He didn't know, of course, but he did know where Hell was — in a corner deep inside his skull.

And he was there right now.

12

One Man's Fury

He stayed on the hill until dark. He was 1000 feet above the river and the surrounding flat land and the only ranch he saw was Clutterbuck's Block C. There were traces that vaguely defined what had once been river-bottom farms but these had obviously been absorbed into Block C long ago. What had happened to the struggling sodbusters who had owned them could be easily guessed at.

By the time sundown faded and night had fallen like a blanket, stars pricking the sky, a hint of moon-rise just fanning a little extra light in the east, Selby had the ten men pin-pointed.

There was a dam just below the lake. It was big for a log construction and it seemed to him that to feed the vast water-hungry country below Conchas that a much larger dam would be needed. In fact, there were signs of excavation on the banks rising each side where provision for future development had been made.

Two men were on guard duty there.

The other eight were in separate positions but he noticed that each man was so placed that he would be able to see signals from any of the others. Clutterbuck was using his ex-army and marshal's experience. He must feel mighty snug and secure back there in the big sprawling log and stone ranch house with its outbuildings placed strategically around it.

Well, a medieval castle wouldn't stop Selby now he had come this far . . .

★ ★ ★

For years, he had carried moccasins in his saddlebags. On more then one occasion they had saved his neck and allowed him to close in silently on his enemies or sneak away like a ghost. He put them on now, checked his hunting knife which was honed razor-sharp, touched every bullet loop on his belt — each was filled, as were the rifle's magazine and the Colt's cylinder.

Time to go.

He had already made up his mind: if Cassie wasn't there, if she had been harmed or, worse, killed, then he would wipe Clutterbuck and Landers off the face of the earth even if he died himself in the process.

A man who is prepared to die by his actions is a formidable man indeed. Clutterbuck and Landers had no idea of what was about to hit them.

The first guard was easy — he was sleeping with a full belly after supper, and his rifle had slipped from his lap where he had placed it. Selby's gun butt between the eyes ensured he would dream on — though whether those dreams were pleasant or nightmares was anybody's guess.

Clay tied the man's wrists behind his

back and bound his ankles and lower legs firmly. He gagged him with cloth torn from the man's own shirt and moved on to where he knew the next guard was stationed.

This one was awake and smoking, the moving bright red dot allowing Selby to home in easily. The guard heard the whisper of the moccasins across rough rock, turned sharply, dropping his cigarette as he fumbled his grip on his rifle. The spray of sparks briefly illuminated a dark shape lunging forward and the man gave a stifled, involuntary cry that was smashed back into his mouth by a clubbing rifle butt.

Selby had similar success with the next two but the man after that was trouble. Clay was working down by the river now, well below the dam, towards the ranch yard. The guard had apparently heard Selby slugging the man up in the rocks above and was waiting below. He had set up his hat on a stick between some rocks and it fooled Selby briefly, but, keyed-up, senses alert to the smallest warning, Clay heard the man's clothing brush the coarse sandstone, spun around as the gun butt whistled down. It glanced off his shoulder and he spilled out of the rocks onto the lush grass. The guard came after him without a sound, a dark shape blurring across the stars, rifle coming around to brace into his hip.

Selby didn't want any shooting, so he rolled towards the man, kicked out at his knees. The guard grunted in pain and his leg buckled. As he fell, still trying to get his rifle into position to shoot, Clay rose like an uncoiling snake and buried his knife blade to the hilt in the man's heart.

Crouching, listening for any more of the guards having been alerted, he wiped the steel on the grass, sheathed the knife and picked up his own guns.

He didn't realize that the next guard was so close — the one he had killed had been out of position, possibly answering a call of nature — and he almost walked into a bullet as he rounded some brush, not expecting to see another guard for some yards yet.

The gun hammered and if the man hadn't tried for a headshot he might have had some success with Clay's upper body silhouetted against the slivery sheen of the river. As it was, it knocked Selby's hat askew and Clay instinctively dropped to one knee, triggering the rifle, levering and firing again. He heard the man crash, thrashing, and was moving at a run to the next position he had pinpointed during the afternoon.

The surprise element was gone now and men were shouting, a gun triggering somewhere but no bullets coming in his direction yet. Then someone yelled, 'I see him! On the river-bank!'

Two slugs kicked into the turf only a yard in front of him and he dived away from the water, getting closer to the rocky slope where the guards were — and where deep shadow would give him cover. But he almost ran into one man who was coming down the slope helter-skelter, likely unable to stop his own momentum, rifle out to one side, yelling some kind of war-whoop. A bullet brought him to an abrupt halt, knocking him flat on his fanny where he lay still after skidding a few more feet.

Clay was moving away, fast, doubled-up, but lead followed him and, still running, still crouched, he braced the rifle butt against one hip, worked lever and trigger until the hammer fell on an empty breech, raking the rocks above. There were snarling ricochets, clatter of rock chips as they erupted from stony surfaces, curses of men — and one heavy grunt, followed closely by a shrill cry. A body came tumbling down, flailing, and Clay didn't duck fast enough. A boot on the end of a limp leg took him across the side of the head and knocked him into a rock. Dazed, he shook his head, lost his grip on the rifle.

Boots were thudding and voices were yelling, but he couldn't make out any words. His vision cleared enough to see three men pounding towards him and his Colt came up as they began shooting. He dropped flat, rolling, shooting, rolling again — away from the rocks. He figured they would expect him to make for the cover of the rocks and the lead that passed over him told him he was right — they were shooting too high now.

He flopped onto his belly, rammed elbows into the grass and picked off two men with his next two shots. He thought maybe one man died but the other was wounded in the hip and screaming blue murder.

The remaining man swore, spun and ran into the night . . .

He couldn't believe his success — mostly through luck, but success anyway. Except all the shooting would have alerted the house.

He had studied the lay-out of the place well during the afternoon, committing to memory the position of the ranch buildings, corrals, blacksmith's forge, cookhouse and so on. He had always had pretty good night vision and he was able to make his way around the corrals where he found a man crouching, his back to Clay, holding a shotgun.

Clay slammed him on the back of the head with the butt of his reloaded rifle, took the shotgun. On his belly, he worked his way towards the house, using elbows and knees, the Greener and Winchester cradled in his crooked arms. There was still light in the house but likely only one lantern turned low, judging by the feeble glow.

He got in close, smelled tobacco and booze, saw a darker-than-dark shape on one end of the porch. Clay eased the rifle away, placed it flat on the ground against the porch's stone foundations, then worked his way around to where the man crouched. With unerring accuracy, Clay drove the butt of the shotgun between the rails into the middle of the man's face and the expelling breath brought another gust of tobacco and booze to him as the man collapsed.

'Cain?' a voice called hoarsely from inside the house, probably just inside the front door.

And it sounded like Rush Landers . . .

'Ok.' Selby murmured, mouth against his forearm to muffle the word. 'Slipped.'

'For Chris'sake stay still!' Landers sounded on edge — *that was good*.

But Clay Selby backed off, made his way down the other side of the house where he could see the dull light spilling through a gap where the window blind had not been pulled all the way down. He heard the murmur of low voices, eased up slowly so he could look through the gap.

The first thing he felt was a wave of relief that almost drowned him.

Cassie was alive!

She was in the room with a man he suspected was Guy Clutterbuck — he hadn't managed a really good look at him that time at Big Bear Rock.

His next feeling was one of shock — shock that felt like dynamite exploding in his belly, numbing, killing every nerve in his body before he was blown apart.

Cassie was alive, certainly. She was sitting in an easy chair, holding out a crystal goblet while Clutterbuck refilled it with red wine, and said, quietly, 'Don't worry, my dear. Rush and the boys will see that Selby doesn't get within a hundred yards of this house.'

And she smiled at the man, said huskily, 'I hope you're right, Guy . . . '

She sipped from the refilled glass of wine, still smiling a little.

★   ★   ★

Selby was stunned — more than stunned. He froze, the incredulity rendering him absolutely helpless for at least thirty seconds.

And that was twenty-nine seconds too long. He realized that when he felt the gun barrel ram brutally against his spine, a hand smashing into the back of his head, slamming his forehead into the logs of the house.

223

There were exploding stars, arcing rockets, rough handling, his aching body bouncing off steps and furniture and finally he was flung, sprawling on his face, on a rug that slid a little across the polished wooden floor where it rested. Moaning once, his head feeling as if it had been kicked by a horse, he rolled onto his back.

'Clay!'

Through blood that was trickling into his eyes from the gash across his forehead, he saw her, wearing that blue dress with the white lace edging, only now it was crumpled and grimy and part of the lace hung loose. She no longer wore the bandage around her head and, although she was pale, she looked better than the last time he had seen her.

'What've you done to him?' she demanded angrily of Rush Landers, who was nudging Selby hard with his boot toe.

'Found him under the window, Guy. He'd stretched out Cain on the porch so I went lookin'.' He drove a boot hard into Selby, moving his body on the rug. 'Got you at last, you son of a bitch!'

'Leave him alone!' snapped Cassie, hands clenched at her sides.

'Shut up,' Landers said, and Guy Clutterbuck now came into the ambit of Clay's vision.

Tall, though slightly stooped at the shoulders, broad, well dressed in pin-striped trousers, loose-sleeved silk shirt, steel-grey streaks in his mop of hair.

'Been a long time, Selby.'

'Not ... long ... enough,' Clay gritted and Clutterbuck laughed briefly.

'Still got some fire in him, Rush.'

'I'll soon quench that!' Landers kicked Selby again and Clutterbuck frowned, grabbed the girl's arm as she made to step forward.

'No,' he said flatly, and Cassie stopped, looking at him with anger blazing in her eyes.

'You said — '

'I just said 'no' and that's what I

mean!' Clutterbuck snapped. 'You sit down — there! — in that chair and hold your tongue. This is my business now.'

Cassie cringed as he lifted a hand in a threatening backhand blow. She nodded, sighing. 'All right, you take over then, but I don't have to watch!'

She started up but Landers shoved her back roughly, teeth bared. 'Yeah you do, lady! You're gonna watch while I shoot him to pieces and then Guy'll do what he wants with him and you'll see every move we make on him!'

Cassie looked sick and slumped in the chair, staring in anguish. But if she expected to see some softening of Clay's blood-streaked face she was mightily disappointed. He looked as if he wanted to kill her with his bare hands.

Clutterbuck was leaning his hips against a heavy carved table now and Landers was opening and closing the fingers of his right hand, rubbing his right shoulder with his left. Ice-cold eyes never left Selby still sprawled on the floor.

'Everythin' OK in there, boss?' a breathless voice called from outside.

'Everything is very much OK, Bull,' Clutterbuck replied, looking and sounding very pleased. 'We've got Selby where we want him. Tell the boys to relax. There'll be no more trouble now.'

'Right, boss.' The man outside sounded a trifle uncertain, but they heard the crunch of gravel under his boots as he went away.

'On your feet!' Landers snapped suddenly, kicking out at Clay who rolled just out of reach. Landers snarled and strode after him, reaching down to lock his fingers in the man's jacket, hauling him upright.

Clay rammed the top of his head into Landers' startled face and the man staggered back, blood flowing from nostrils and mouth, already reaching for his gun.

Cassie screamed and Clutterbuck

yelled, rolling back across the table, dropping to the floor.

The room shook to the sound of gunfire as the six-guns exploded. Selby was wrenched around violently as Landers slammed back into the wall. Clay's gun fired twice more and Landers dropped to his knees, coughing scarlet blood. He tried to talk but Clay Selby straightened, taking his hand away from the wound that had clipped his upper chest, passing through. 'Too slow, Rush — way too slow.'

Landers' eyes flared with one final burst of impotent anger and he fell forward on his face.

'Clay!'

Cassie's scream knifed through Selby's ringing senses and, instincts working at incredible speed, he twisted and went down to one knee in the same movement, smoking pistol coming up. He fired across the table at Clutterbuck who had a blazing gun in his hand.

The ex-marshal lifted to his toes, tried to fire again, but Clay's last bullet took him in the wide chest and smashed him into the wall. His upper body jarred violently across the end of the heavy table and he rolled off to sprawl half-sitting, in the angle of the wall. His jaw was slack as he tried to look down at the blood-oozing wound.

Cassie started to help Clay to his feet but he shook free savagely and thrust her from him. Her eyes widened. 'Clay!'

'Get away from me!' he rasped, swaying a little as he fumbled to reload the six-gun.

'Boss? Boss?' The same voice as before called from out in the yard and Selby went around the table fast, hauled Clutterbuck to his feet and held him upright. He pressed the hot muzzle of his six-gun against the man's head.

'Tell him it's OK!'

Clutterbuck had to fight for breath but, with a little more pressure from the Colt's barrel, called harshly, 'Dammit! Told you we had it under control, Bull! Now — get!'

'OK, boss,' came the reluctant reply,

after a hesitation.

Clay heaved Clutterbuck up onto the table, stood over him, completing the reloading of his Colt as he looked down at the man.

'You're all through, Clutterbuck — you're a tough man, but you're finished now.'

'Clay, don't . . . ' started Cassie, but one withering look from him stopped her in her tracks.

'You shut up — I've got nothing to say to you.'

'But — ' Whatever else she was going to say died and then she seemed to make a physical effort, straightening her shoulders, tilting her jaw in that stubborn way she had.

'Why?' she demanded, and the flat, no-nonsense tone made him snap his head up.

He was wadding a kerchief over his wound now as he met her angry gaze. 'You still haven't forgiven me for running out on you twelve years ago, have you?' he said bitterly.

She frowned. 'Is that what you think?'

'Hell! *Think?* I was too damn dumb, too damn pleased to have you back — or thought I did — to see further than the tip of my own stupid nose!'

'I told you that wire to Clutterbuck was a mistake — we — we talked about it! We said we loved each other!'

He snorted. 'Love? Another stupid word I added to my vocabulary and I let it blind me. Judas, Cassie, I saw you drinking wine with Clutterbuck! Heard you say you hoped his men would keep me away from this house! It all came together then: you were gone from Brodie's, and like Yankee Bill and everyone else, I figured Landers had grabbed you as a hostage. After he'd strung-up Karen Brodie, he needed someone else in case he was cornered — *and to lead me here where he had plenty of help to get me!* Your help. You went along with him, saw your big chance to square with me for what you reckoned was my having jilted you back in Patchett.'

Cassie turned slowly and sat down in the easy chair. She folded her hands in her lap, seemed pale but calm enough as she studied his gaunt, pain-racked face. And she knew it wasn't all physical pain.

'I suppose it could look that way. In fact, it was the way I wanted it to look. For Landers' benefit and Clutterbuck's. I thought if I let them think I was nothing more than a hostage, I'd never be able to help you in some way. Landers'd tie me up or beat me — maybe even rape me — but if he thought I hated you and had waited as long as he had to get back at you, then he was smart enough to see the advantage of it. Let you think I was in real danger and nothing would stop you coming. I swear to you, Clay, that's how it was! I did it so I'd have a chance to — to *help*!'

Her control broke at last on the final word. She drew in a shuddering breath

232

and then the tears flowed and her shoulders shook as she buried her face in her hands.

Clay Selby felt churned up, strung out, as if he was standing on his head — full of all kinds of emotions and odd feelings.

By God, he wanted to believe her! Wanted nothing more on this earth right now — to believe she loved him enough to risk her very life for him that way . . .

Clutterbuck coughed blood as Clay started forward, paused and looked back at the wounded man. He was surprised to see the man's lips pulled back in a sneer.

'Stupid fool!' the man gasped, coughing more blood.

Clay ignored him, went to stand by Cassie's chair. The dull light glinted from her raven-dark hair and his hand shook a little as he reached out to touch it.

'Cassie,' he said, quietly, throat as dry as a sand dune.

She kept sobbing, then it gradually eased and she looked up at him with wet, reddened eyes. Slowly she reached up and closed a hand over his where it rested on her head.

He pulled her to her feet and she came in against him, arms going about him in a grip with much more strength in it than he would have expected.

Her face pressed against his chest and her grip was hurting his fresh wound but he bit back the moan that wanted to escape him as she stepped back an inch and looked up at him.

'Oh, Clay, I — I do love you so!'

He swallowed. 'I reckon you've proved that, Cassie. I was a blamed fool, thinking you'd turned on me — '

Her finger touched his lips, silencing him. 'It's all right, Clay. You've had hard times and you've had to react in a hard way, but those times are over now — we're together and we'll stay that way from now on.'

There was coughing from the table and blood sprayed into the air and then there was a strange sound that Selby thought at first was the death rattle. It made him stiffen when he saw that Clutterbuck's ghastly face was turned towards them, the man's mouth in a rictus that could have been a dying smile. The sound was an attempt at laughter!

'F-fools!' he croaked. 'You think Hannigan'll let you live? After hunting for you all this time . . . ? You've cost him thousands — trying to track you down, Selby. He can't let you live now. *Can't*. He's gonna be Governor. You'll never reach him. Bodyguards . . . by the dozen. But he'll get you . . . he'll get you . . . '

'I'll just have to kill him first, won't I?' Clay Selby said, as one final spasm racked Clutterbuck and he died, sliding off the table with a thud.

Cassie's face was horrified, but she wasn't looking at Clutterbuck, she was staring at Selby.

* ★ ★

There was a man waiting for them outside, likely the one who had called twice to make sure everything was all right earlier. The one Clutterbuck had called Bull.

There was a movement as they came around the rear of the house, and the man stepped out from cover, saying, 'Knew the boss sounded different! Uh-uh! You take it easy, Selby! I got that shotgun you left under the window. Now let's move to the porch and go inside and see what kinda hell you made in there.'

They began moving and the man, a squat but solid-looking figure in the night, said as they stumbled down the side of the house, 'You be a lot tougher'n they figured, huh?'

'Be quiet!' snapped the girl angrily, arm about the bent-over Selby. 'He's wounded and can hardly stand.'

The man snorted. 'Well, won't be long before he's restin', lady — for a long, long time. Hey!'

Clay stumbled by the end of the

porch, going down to one knee, almost pulling the girl off her feet. He pushed her aside with one hand, scooped up the rifle he had left there with his other, cocking the hammer smoothly as he rolled. The man with the shotgun hadn't even bothered to cock the hammers and that small oversight cost him his life.

The rifle whiplashed, jumped in Clay's one-handed grip and before the man crumpled, he had another shell levered in and hammered him down with a second shot. The Greener skidded across the gravel.

'Help me up, Cass!' he gritted. 'Don't think there's anyone else close, but the gunfire'll likely bring in someone eventually.'

She hesitated, then helped him struggle up and, as they made their way to the corrals, she said in a kind of shocked voice, 'You *are* a killer, aren't you?'

He stopped briefly, surprised, but stumbled on again quickly.

'If I am they made me one.'

'You can't possibly go after Tate Hannigan!' Cassie was adamant and she almost stamped her foot for more emphasis.

Wearily, for the twentieth time he said, 'I have to, Cass, you know I do.'

'But — but it's suicide! You heard what Clutterbuck said: Tate Hannigan is surrounded by dozens of bodyguards!'

'I heard that, sure, but what I heard most of all was that no matter what, Hannigan is gonna keep sending men after me until someone kills me — and he'll kill you, too, now, because you know what I know.'

She looked exasperated, but at the same time he saw that his words had hit home. 'Clay, there's been enough killing. Maybe it's my Quaker upbringing, but I — I can't condone any more. Especially as you know you couldn't be successful!' This time she did stamp her foot. They were in a hotel room in a place called Santo Domingo, south of

Santa Fe — where Hannigan was, according to Cassie, who had heard Landers telling Clutterbuck. There was thick carpet on the floor and her stamping foot did little to emphasize her arguments. 'How can you even think of going when you know how well he'll be guarded? It's — it's so foolish!'

'Cassie, I was taught to shoot by a man who was one of Berdan's Sharpshooters in the war. I know how to tune my rifle so I can get a head shot in at maximum range. I can kill him and be away before his guards know what's happened.'

His words trailed off as he saw the horror on her face. She backed away from him.

'You're talking about cold-blooded murder!' she gasped.

'Just what Hannigan has planned for us! For God's sake, Cass, use your head! If I don't do this, we'll never know a moment's peace for the rest of our days — and they likely wouldn't be many.'

She kept shaking her head as he spoke, saying 'No! No! No!'

His belly was tied in a cold knot. He didn't want to chance his life again, but he knew he had to. There was no other way. As long as Hannigan lived, they were both targets. If he didn't make it back, that was too bad — not the way he'd like it, but at least he would know she would be safe as long as he managed to kill Hannigan.

And that was all that mattered now!

It came to him coldly and he felt a kind of relaxation even though what he was going to do would tear him apart. *He would lose her even if he survived, but at least she would be alive and no longer threatened.*

'Cassie, I'm going to kill Hannigan. I have to.'

There were tears in her eyes as she looked up into his face, silent for a long minute. Then she said, a little shakily, but with that strongly thrusting jaw, 'I won't be here when — if — you come back, Clay.'

'Cass, try to see that what I'm saying is the only way.'

Again her head was shaking even as he pleaded.

'I can't condone murder, Clay! You must see that!'

He sighed and nodded. 'I see it, Cass, and I respect your views, but I still have to do it if we're to have any kind of a life together.'

'You — I meant it, Clay! I won't be here and if ever you find me, I'll have nothing to do with you!'

He nodded.

She would be safe. That was all that mattered.

He set his hat on his head, picked up his rifle and warbag and paused briefly at the door.

'*Adios*, Cass,' he said and went out.

Her sobbing followed him along the passage almost to the head of the stairs that led down to the foyer and beyond, to the long trail ahead of him that would only end with the sound of gunfire.